N234b

Bernie and the Bessledorf Ghost

Books by Phyllis Reynolds Naylor

Witch's Sister
Witch Water
The Witch Herself
Walking Through the Dark
How I Came to Be a Writer
How Lazy Can You Get?
Eddie, Incorporated
All Because I'm Older
Shadows on the Wall
Faces in the Water
Footprints at the Window
The Boy with the Helium Head
A String of Chances
The Solomon System
The Mad Gasser of Bessledorf Street
Night Cry
Old Sadie and the Christmas Bear
The Dark of the Tunnel
The Agony of Alice
The Keeper
The Bodies in the Bessledorf Hotel
The Year of the Gopher
Beetles, Lightly Toasted
Maudie in the Middle
One of the Third Grade Thonkers
Alice in Rapture, Sort of
Keeping a Christmas Secret
Bernie and the Bessledorf Ghost

Bernie and the Bessledorf Ghost

Phyllis Reynolds Naylor

A Jean Karl Book

Atheneum   1990   New York

Atheneum
Macmillan Publishing Company
866 Third Avenue, New York, NY 10022
Collier Macmillan Canada, Inc.
First Edition
Printed in the United States of America   .
10 9 8 7 6 5 4 3 2 1

Library of Congress Cataloging-in-Publication Data
Naylor, Phyllis Reynolds.
Bernie and the Bessledorf ghost/Phyllis Reynolds Naylor.
—1st ed.   p.   cm.
"A Jean Karl book."
Summary: Living at the Bessledorf Hotel, where his father works as
the manager, Bernie tries to solve the mystery of a troubled young
ghost who wanders the halls of the hotel at night.
ISBN 0-689-31499-X
[1. Ghosts—Fiction.   2. Mystery and detective stories.
3. Hotels, motels, etc.—Fiction.]   I. Title.
PZ7.N24Bg   1990   [Fic]—dc19
88-29389   CIP   AC

To Hayden Reiss,
whose father likes these books,
and to Amtrak—
on which this book was written

Contents

Bernie and the Bessledorf Ghost

1

At the Foot
of the Bed

The Bessledorf Hotel was at 600 Bessledorf Street, between the bus depot and the funeral parlor. Officer Feeney said that some folks came into town on one side of the hotel and exited on the other. The Bessledorf had thirty rooms, not counting the apartment where Bernie Magruder's family lived, and Feeney said that a ghost could be in a room—even a room at the Bessledorf—and you might not even know it.

Bernie had brought the subject up. He asked Feeney whether or not he believed in ghosts.

"Don't know whether I do or don't, since I never saw one to speak of," the officer told him. " 'Course, a ghost could lean over your shoulder and eat off your plate and the only thing you'd notice, like as not, was a little draft about the head." And then he stopped swinging his nightstick and looked straight at Bernie. "Why?"

"Because my sister has dreamed about a ghost three nights in a row now, and she's worried."

"What's this ghost look like?" asked Feeney.

"She says he's about eleven, like me."

"Well, now, years ago, before I came on the force, actually, I heard talk of ghosts at the Bessledorf, but that's all it was. Just talk. 'Course, that hotel *is* an old one, you know. What does this ghost do in your sister's dream?"

"Delores says he just walks in and stands there."

Feeney chuckled. "That's the most harmless-sounding ghost I ever heard of. Tell her to drink a nice glass of warm milk before she goes to bed. If that's the worst dream she ever has, she's lucky."

It had been a disturbing week at the Bessledorf. Mrs. Magruder had decided that the hotel needed some repairs that just couldn't wait. The leaky roof, for example, that dripped down on old Mr. Lamkin, one of the regulars. The broken window in the attic that let in an occasional bat. And she had put up with the dirt floor in the cellar long enough, she declared, and pleaded with Mr. Fairchild, the owner, to lay a new one of cement.

And because the Magruders, Theodore and Alma,

had been good managers, and because their four children—Delores, Joseph, Bernie, and Lester—had been obedient, and because the family pets—Mixed Blessing, the Great Dane; Lewis and Clark, the cats; and Salt Water, the parrot—had not bitten or otherwise disgusted the Bessledorf's guests unduly, Mr. Fairchild had had the roof fixed, the windows repaired, and had sent a cement truck around. At last the Magruders had a roof that didn't leak, an attic window that wasn't broken, and a cellar floor they could walk on without tripping over the lumps and bumps and getting their socks dirty.

The dust had hardly cleared, however, before it was discovered that Lewis, the smaller of the cats, was missing. The family was terrified that perhaps he had been in the cellar when the cement came pouring in and would stay there forever, a mere statue of a cat. When they went to check, they accidentally let the other animals in, too, and while Mixed Blessing chased Clark around over the wet concrete, Salt Water flew above, flapping and squawking, and when the floor had dried at last, it was dotted here and there with paw prints and feathers. Lewis had been asleep in a box in the alley all the time.

"It's a good thing Mr. Fairchild lives in Indianapolis, not Middleburg," said Bernie's father, "or we would all be out on the street."

No sooner were these repairs done, however, than

stairs that had only creaked before were discovered to have loose banisters as well, and the carpeting in the lobby that had looked merely frayed only a few months ago now came perilously close to being shabby.

"Well, what can you expect of a one-hundred-twenty-five-year-old hotel?" said Theodore. "It is exactly the way an old hotel should look; that's what gives it charm."

Things would have been a lot neater, of course, without the pets. It was Joseph who brought them home. Joseph was in college studying to be a veterinarian, and when first Mixed Blessing, then Lewis and Clark, and finally Salt Water were left unwanted in baskets on the veterinary college steps, it was Joseph who brought them home to the Bessledorf.

When things were tense around the hotel, however, and people were upset, four animals in the place did not help. Delores, who was twenty and worked up the street in the parachute factory, was especially upset because the ghost dreams had been disturbing her sleep, and she wanted so much to be named Worker of the Week at the factory. The Worker of the Week was given her own parking space for a week, her own special cup at the coffee machine, and a twenty-five-dollar bonus. For the last month Delores had been going to work early, leaving late, and sewing straps and pounding grommets just as fast as she could to impress her supervisor.

But the ghost dreams made her irritable, and one evening, when she came to the dinner table, it seemed that whatever anyone did upset her.

"Don't wipe your fingers on your T-shirt, Lester," Delores said grumpily. "And you don't have to belch out loud, either."

"Would you pass the butter, Joseph, or are you deaf?" she snapped.

"Mother, you *know* I don't like stewed tomatoes," she continued.

Bernie, who was silently eating his mashed potatoes, asked finally, "Am I chewing too loud for you, Delores?"

"My nerves are frayed to a frazzle!" Delores said. "If anyone drops a fork, I'll scream."

Lester dropped a fork, and Delores screamed.

"Well, you're not the only one who's had a hard day," Mrs. Magruder complained. Bernie's mother wrote romance novels in her spare time, and her latest, *Quivering Lips*, had just been rejected. "You're not the only one in the world with problems."

"My dear, dear family," said Theodore, from his chair at the head of the table. "It is a beautiful evening in June and far too lovely to be spent squibbling here at the table."

"Squabbling," his wife said.

"I want each of you, when the meal is over," Father continued, "to go to your room and contemplate how lucky we are that we have a roof over our heads, food on our table, and clothes on our backs, and that none of us—at the moment, anyway—is lying in the funeral parlor next door. If that doesn't make you grateful, you should hang your heads in shame."

Delores reached for the last sticky bun on the table. "What if I dream of that ghost again tonight?"

"Officer Feeney says to drink a glass of warm milk and that will stop it," Bernie suggested helpfully.

Delores sniffed. "I'd like to know what *Feeney* drinks before he goes to bed, and I'll bet it's not milk."

The Magruders' apartment was behind the registration desk in the lobby. It was a large apartment with four bedrooms, and Bernie shared one of them with Lester.

Lying on the top bunk and thinking about what his father had said, Bernie knew that his dad was right. They really did have a lot to be thankful for. This was the first place Mr. Magruder had worked for more than a few years at a time, and Bernie loved Middleburg and the friends he had made. He hoped they could live in the Bessledorf always, and he didn't care a bit that it was one of the oldest buildings in Middleburg.

But maybe for some people—Delores, for example—that wasn't enough. She wasn't happy with just a roof over her head and a good job at the parachute factory. She wanted to be Worker of the Week as well.

Even Mother had dreams of someday writing a best-seller and having her name known in bookstores across the country. Well, there was nothing wrong with that. Everyone wanted to be, if not exactly famous, at least remembered. Bernie himself had dreams occasionally of getting his name in the *Guinness Book of World Records* for coasting the longest distance on a skateboard.

"Lightning bugs," said Lester from the bunk below.

Bernie looked toward the window. He didn't see any.

"Roller skates," said Lester.

Bernie listened, but he didn't hear anyone skating.

"Bubble gum . . . bicycles . . . peanut butter . . ." Lester went on.

"What the heck are you doing?" Bernie asked.

"Counting our blessings, like Dad said. Marshmallow sundaes . . . Reeboks . . . Ring Dings . . . transistor radios . . ."

Bernie got up and went out on the front step to watch the moon come up. Slowly the traffic on the street began to thin, lights went out in the funeral parlor, guests came in from off the street where they had gone to take an evening stroll, and behind him, in the lobby, Father began locking up—checking the windows, pulling the drapes, and turning the key in the cash register.

Bernie came in at last and crawled back into bed.

He could hear Lester's steady breathing in the bunk below, the sound of Mixed Blessing scratching himself outside the bedroom door, his collar jangling. The silence of night closed in around him—no more faucets turning on and off, no more opening and closing of the elevator door. Bernie turned over, burying one ear in his pillow, and closed his eyes. He probably slept for an hour or two. Maybe longer. But suddenly the air was split with a most horrible scream.

Bernie rose up, listening, his heart pounding.

"W-what was *that?*" came Lester's voice from below.

Bernie slid his legs over the side of the bunk and dropped to the floor. "It sounded like Delores," he said, and went out in the hall in his pajamas.

Joseph was there, and Mother and Father, as well, all staring at Delores, who was leaning against the wall, her eyes the size of eggs.

"It . . . it wasn't just a dream!" she gasped. "It was real! The ghost! Standing right there at the foot of my bed."

2

Now You See Him, Now You Don't

"Delores, my girl," said Mr. Magruder, "are you *sure* you weren't dreaming?"

Delores could hardly speak. "I had j-just come back from the kitchen, Dad, with a glass of warm milk; I'd crawled into bed and was sipping the milk slowly when I . . . I saw him."

"What happened then?"

"I screamed, and he disappeared. Oh, it was terrible!"

"How do you know it was a ghost and not a real person?" asked Joseph.

"B-because," said Delores, and her teeth were chattering again, "just before he appeared, I felt a cold draft, and when he stood at the foot of the bed, I could see right through him—a chair, my closet. . . . It's just as if he was fog."

"Well, I'll put a stop to this," said Bernie's father. "Delores, you sleep with your mother tonight, and *I* will sleep in your bedroom. Now everyone go back to bed before we wake the guests."

Bernie could hardly believe that the scream had not awakened everyone else in the hotel already. Felicity Jones, one of the regulars, usually awoke at the slightest sound. Mrs. Buzzwell could spread rumors more quickly than a strong wind, and whenever Felicity Jones and Mrs. Buzzwell got going, they managed to upset old Mr. Lamkin, as well.

For a long time Bernie lay on his bed whispering to his nine-year-old brother below.

"What do you suppose the ghost wants?" Bernie mused.

"Maybe he's hungry," said Lester.

"Ghosts don't eat, Lester."

"Maybe he's tired and wants to lie down."

"So why doesn't he use the couch in the lobby?"

"Well, *I* don't know, Bernie. But you won't find *me* sleeping in that bedroom. Not for all the money in the world."

Bernie felt the same way. "If someone's playing a trick on us, Dad will find out," he said, and finally he fell asleep.

The following morning, however, Mr. Magruder said that he had never slept better in his life, and that he had not been awakened even once, and he was sure it was all in his daughter's imagination.

"Ah, Mrs. Buzzwell!" he said at the registration desk as the heavyset woman came through the lobby on her way to breakfast. "A lovely morning, isn't it?"

"It is *not*!" Mrs. Buzzwell snapped. "That was the worst night's sleep I have ever had. There was a *draft*, Mr. Magruder. I don't know where it came from, but there was a draft."

"I'm sorry to hear that," said Bernie's father. "I'll have Mr. Wilkins check out your room, of course."

Old Mr. Lamkin came through the lobby next. "Not a bone in my body that doesn't ache," he told Bernie. "Last three nights I've tossed and turned. Couldn't get comfortable no matter what."

"Maybe tonight will be better," Bernie offered, and turned the television to the "Today" show, which Mr. Lamkin liked to watch over his morning coffee.

When Felicity Jones came through, she had a shawl draped over her head and around her shoulders, and there were dark circles beneath her eyes, even though she was still a very young woman.

"Felicity, my dear, are you ill?" asked Mother.

"I'm so cold," Felicity said. "So very cold."

"But it's seventy-eight degrees outside," said Mother. "It's almost the first day of summer!"

"I know," said Felicity. "I can't explain it myself. But in here it's like a tomb. All cold and damp and drafty."

Bernie saw his parents exchange worried glances.

As soon as he'd had his breakfast, Bernie went outside to the alley and climbed up on the wall to wait for his two best friends, Georgene Riley and Weasel. Georgene wore her long hair in a ponytail that hung halfway down her back, and Weasel wore glasses that kept sliding down his nose. As soon as his friends had hoisted themselves up on the brick wall beside him, Bernie told them the news: "We've got ghosts," he said.

Georgene and Weasel stared at him.

"I've heard of people having mice or roaches, but not ghosts," said Georgene. "How do you know? Do doors keep opening or something?"

"Delores saw one at the foot of her bed."

"Is she *sure?*" asked Weasel, pushing his glasses up once again.

"Pretty sure. Dad slept in her room last night, though, and he didn't see a thing."

"What did it look like? What did it say?" Georgene wanted to know.

"It looked like a boy about eleven years old, and he didn't say anything. Just stood there."

"That doesn't sound like any kind of ghost I ever heard of," said Weasel. "They're at least supposed to go 'hoo' and rattle their chains or something."

"Well, this one didn't have any chains and Delores said she could see right through him like a fog," Bernie told them.

Georgene looked around warily. "Maybe one got loose from over there," she said, nodding toward the funeral parlor on the other side of the hotel.

"What do you mean, 'got loose'?" Bernie asked.

"I mean the part of you that was alive before. Maybe it got lost on its way to heaven," Georgene explained.

"So what do you want me to do?" Bernie said. "Put a sign on Delores's bedroom saying HEAVEN, with an arrow pointing up?"

"I think we should find out if any boys about eleven years old have died recently and have been embalmed there at the funeral home," said Georgene.

"That's just great," said Bernie. "I'm supposed to go the funeral parlor and ask what's new?"

"Not if it bothers you," said Georgene. "I'll do it."

She slid down off the wall, and while Bernie and Weasel stared in astonishment, Georgene walked across the gravel lot of the funeral home, up the back steps, and knocked on the door.

Bernie couldn't hear what she was saying, but he saw the back door open, saw a man in a black suit come out on the step, saw Georgene say something, and saw the man shake his head.

"All they've had for the past week is an eighty-year-old woman, one baby, one forty-seven-year-old man, and a grandfather. No boys at all," Georgene said when she returned.

"I'll bet it was all a dream," said Weasel. "If there was a ghost prowling around Delores's room every night, your dad would have seen it."

"Not necessarily," said Bernie. "Dad's a heavy sleeper. He could sleep through anything."

That night, when the Magruders gathered again for dinner, Mrs. Magruder must have been thinking the same thing, because when the subject of ghosts came up and Theodore declared that there weren't any, she said, "Theodore, you would sleep through an earthquake."

"Then I shall sleep there again tonight with one eye open," Bernie's father declared, but when Bernie passed the bedroom about midnight on his way to get a glass of water, he could hear his father snoring loudly and knew that the ghost could be sitting beside the bed playing a harmonica and his father would never know.

Sure enough, the following night, when Delores

went back to her own room, the family was awakened again about three by a small, muffled scream. Again they descended on Delores's room—all in their nightclothes—and found her sitting up in bed, clutching the sheet to her throat, her face as white as cotton. She was pointing to the foot of her bed. But the space was empty. There was nothing to see but a closet and a chair. Bernie noticed, however, that the room was strangely chilly for a warm night in June, as though a cold wind had just blown through.

"Oh, Delores, my darling!" said Mother, throwing her arms around her daughter. "Was it here again?"

"R-right where it was before, Mother. It didn't move, didn't speak, just stood there looking at me sadly."

"Well, at least we know he hasn't come to harm you," said Theodore. "The important thing is not to let any of our guests find out about this."

Mrs. Magruder glared at her husband. "The *important* thing, Theodore, is to allow our daughter a good night's sleep so that her health will not fail."

"The *important* thing," wailed Delores, "is that I get enough sleep to get to work early so I can do a good job and get to be the Worker of the Week at the parachute factory! How can I sleep with a ghost prowling around the foot of my bed?"

"I wonder what it means," said Joseph. "I wonder what the ghost wants."

And suddenly Mrs. Magruder gave a small cry, grabbed Bernie, and clutched him to her breast. "It's an omen!" she cried. "I just know it! He's come for my Bernie, and I won't let him go!"

3

Joseph's Turn

It was not that Bernie had not thought of that himself. He just had not put it into words, and hearing his mother say those words aloud did not make him feel a bit better.

"Now, Alma," said Mr. Magruder. "The fact that our Delores here thinks she has seen an eleven-year-old ghost does not necessarily mean that he has come for our Bernie."

"Then what has he come for?" asked Mother.

"We don't even know that he's come! We're not even sure that he's been! The only one who has seen this so-called ghost is Delores, and her head has been so full of grommets that she may, if you'll forgive me, be suffering delusions."

Delores gave a little moan and leaned weakly against her mother. Mrs. Magruder stopped hugging Bernie and began hugging Delores again instead.

"I've got it," said Joseph. "I'm a light sleeper, so *I'll* sleep in Delores's room tonight and see what's what."

So Joseph went to bed in Delores's room, and Delores slept with Mother, and Theodore went to sleep in Joseph's room, while Mixed Blessing settled down outside the room where Bernie and Lester had their bunks.

Bernie had to admit he was scared. He was the only eleven-year-old in the hotel, and when an eleven-year-old ghost appears in a bedroom, it must mean something. What if it meant that Bernie was going to fall out of bed that night and break his neck? What if it meant he might choke on a doughnut at breakfast the next morning? What if it meant that his skateboard would go out of control someday on the sidewalk in front of the hotel, and that he would end up in the funeral parlor next door? Bernie shivered beneath his sheet, and the room wasn't even cold. Could it be that the ghost had come already?

The clock in the lobby chimed midnight, then one, then two, then three. . . . And then Mixed Blessing gave a low, low growl outside the bedroom door, and Bernie slid quietly down off the top bunk and opened the door. In the light from the bathroom window, he could see the Great Dane cowering against the wall, whimpering pitifully. Bernie went out to pat him, and the dog nuzzled beneath Bernie's arm, as if to hide.

Bernie walked on down the hall, and when he got to the door of Delores's room, he heard someone talking inside. He stopped, his heart pounding.

"W-who are you?" he heard Joseph saying. "What do you want?"

Bernie froze. He heard the floor creak, saw the doorknob of Delores's room begin to turn. His heart beat so hard beneath his pajamas that he thought it would leap right out of his chest. Then the door swung open. There stood Joseph, looking very pale.

"It's there! The ghost!" Joseph whispered, glad to see Bernie. "Look!"

Bernie swallowed and peeped inside the door. But there was no ghost, only a pale plume of light, fading slowly at the foot of the bed. Mixed Blessing howled mournfully.

By now the whole family was up once again.

"What did the ghost look like, Joseph?" asked his mother. "What did it say?"

"Just as Delores told us," Joseph answered. "It's a boy about Bernie's age—sort of a square face, light hair. I asked who he was, but he didn't answer, and when I asked what he wanted, he . . ."

"What?" Delores asked. "*What*, Joseph?"

"He just raised his hands up in the air like this," said Joseph, and slowly thrust both arms above his head.

"Looks like a stickup," said Lester. "Maybe he's trying to tell us that the hotel's about to be robbed."

"Ridiculous," said Theodore. "My dear children, you are letting your imaginations get the best of you. If there is a young ghost here at the Bessledorf Hotel, he has done no harm that I can see except disturb our sleep, and if Delores would simply ignore him, perhaps that would be the end of it."

"I'd like to see *you* ignore him if he were standing at the foot of *your* bed and you knew it!" Delores snapped. "But that's okay, Dad. If you don't want your daughter to be Worker of the Week, if you want her so pale and bedraggled from lack of sleep that she can't even think, then, no, a ghost on the loose doesn't matter."

"Now, Sweets," said Theodore. "Your father is not going to allow you to worry yourself to pieces. Somehow we will get to the bottom of this and you will have your own bed back before long."

"So who's going to sleep in it next?" Delores asked.

"Not my Bernie!" Mother said, letting go of Delores and grabbing Bernie.

"Don't look at me," said Lester.

"Well, I'm certainly not going to sleep in there," said Mother.

"I'll try again," said Joseph. "Maybe I can find out something more tomorrow night."

It was the first thing Bernie talked about when he and Georgene and Weasel went skateboarding the next morning on Bessledorf Hill. He waited until they had coasted clear to the bottom, fifty yards beyond the funeral home, and then he told them.

Georgene looked worried. "Maybe your mom's right, Bernie," she said. "Maybe the ghost *has* come for you."

"So what's he doing in Delores's room?" Bernie asked. "Why doesn't he come in mine?"

"Maybe he's got a poor sense of direction," Weasel suggested.

"Maybe you should . . ." Georgene began.

"No," Bernie interrupted.

"Just for a night, maybe?"

"Don't even think it," said Bernie.

"But how else will you ever know?"

"We'll see what Joseph finds out tonight," Bernie told her.

That night, none of the Magruders was able to sleep. Delores said that sometimes the ghost came as early as midnight, but sometimes not until three o'clock. The family sat down in the hallway outside Delores's room, waiting—Theodore in his blue-striped night-shirt, Mother in her lavender gown, Delores in her baby-doll pajamas, Bernie in his red shorts, and Lester in his Snoopy pj's.

"I wish he'd hurry and come." Lester yawned.

"There is absolutely no reason in the world for us all to be sitting out here," said Father. "There is no reason whatsoever, Lester, that you can't be in your own bed."

"I don't want to miss anything," Lester said. "If Bernie gets carried off, I want to wave, at least."

"The only thing you will miss, my boy, is a good night's sleep," said Father. "And that goes for the rest of you, too."

Nobody moved.

Mixed Blessing laid his head in Lester's lap. Lester leaned against Bernie, Bernie leaned against Delores, Delores leaned against Mother, Mother leaned against Father, and Theodore said that if anyone sneezed, they would all fall over like dominoes.

At two-fifteen, the bed springs squeaked in Delores's room. Father sat up straight, then Mother, then Delores, then Bernie, then Lester. Mixed Blessing gave a low growl, and then began to whimper. There seemed to be a cold draft in the hallway.

"Who are you?" came Joseph's voice from behind the door. "If you could tell me what you want, perhaps we could help you."

Suddenly a door opened in the opposite direction, and Bernie whirled around. A young woman holding a lighted candle was coming through the door of the Magruders' apartment. It was Felicity Jones in her nightgown. She stared at the Magruder family, sitting in a row in their hallway, and then at the door to Delores's room.

"Mr. Magruder," she said, "I feel an unworldly presence here in the hotel, and I shall not sleep until it is removed from the premises."

Theodore sighed. "Welcome to the club," he said, just as the bedroom door opened and Joseph came out. Joseph stared at Felicity Jones and then at his family. His shoulders slumped.

"He wouldn't talk," Joseph told them. "The ghost said nothing. Nothing at all."

4

A Little Something about Spirits

Bernie figured that if anyone in the hotel should know about ghosts, it was Felicity Jones, because she looked like one herself. She was thin and pale by nature, and Father said that one was never quite sure whether Felicity was in this world or out of it. She read books about spirits, wrote poems about spirits, so the Magruders decided to tell her everything.

"Each night, for the past week," Delores explained, "this ghost, about Bernie's age, has been appearing at the foot of my bed."

Felicity, who had crouched down beside them in the hall, leaned forward, her pale eyes wide. "Does he *ever* talk?" she asked.

"Not a word," said Joseph, wearily. "Just stands there looking mournful and raises his arms."

"His arms?"

"Like this," said Joseph, and stretched his arms above his head.

"Hark!" said Felicity suddenly, listening intently.

Bernie listened, too, but he couldn't hear a thing. He could feel something, though—a cold draft coming from Delores's bedroom. He got to his feet. The cold draft seemed to be moving, and Bernie moved along with it.

"Bernie, my boy, my child, come back!" cried Mother.

Down the hall they went, Bernie and the draft, through the door of the apartment and into the lobby. Mixed Blessing cowered against the wall, the cats began to meow, and Salt Water, the parrot, who should have been asleep, squawked loudly from beneath the blanket covering his cage.

Across the lobby Bernie went. He could tell which way the draft was going, because he felt it on his legs. He could hear the family coming down the hall after him and out into the lobby. Bernie followed the draft as far as the stairs leading up to the second floor, and then it was gone.

"Bernie, don't go!" Theodore called, and then even he sounded worried.

"I just wanted to see where it was going, that's all," Bernie said.

"Whatever can this mean?" asked Mother.

"Felicity, my dear," said Father, "what can you tell us about the behavior of ghosts?"

"Mr. Magruder," said Felicity, "if you want to learn about spirits, come quickly. All of you."

The Magruders followed the young woman back to the apartment kitchen.

"Sit down at the table," said Felicity Jones. "Everyone must put both hands on the table, sit quietly, and not make a sound."

Bernie and Lester exchanged excited glances. This sounded like fun. Chairs were shuffled about, pajamas adjusted, feet put into place. Finally the family was settled around the table. Felicity set her candle in the middle of it and turned out the light.

"Rest your fingers lightly—very lightly—on the table," she instructed, taking her place beside Joseph. "If the ghost is in this room with us, you should feel the table vibrate. And if we can get him into this room, perhaps he will answer by knocking on the table."

Bernie felt Mixed Blessing slink between his chair and Lester's and lie down at their feet. Not even the dog wanted to stay back out in the hallway alone.

In a low, soft voice, Felicity Jones began:

"Ghost of boy
So stiff and cold,
Let his story
Now be told."

Bernie waited. He could feel Lester's hand next to his own, shaking just a little. Everyone waited. Bernie could even hear his dad's breathing across the table.

All at once Bernie felt the table tremble just a little beneath his fingertips. He looked around the circle. At first he thought it might be Lester, shaking with fright. Felicity looked eagerly about the room. The trembling went on, becoming more and more noticeable, and then Bernie realized it was only Mixed Blessing scratching himself beneath the table. He nudged the dog with his foot and the shaking stopped.

Felicity tried again:

"Moon of midnight,
Sage and seer,
Let the ghost-boy
Now appear."

There was a knock on the table.

"Hark!" Felicity said.

"Shhhh," Mother said to the others.

"Ghost-boy," said Felicity Jones, "if you have a message for us, please tap once."

"Thump, thump, thump," went the knocking.

"What?" Felicity pleaded. "Ghost-boy, I don't understand you."

"It's only Mixed Blessing scratching for fleas," Bernie told them.

"Oh, for Pete's sake," said Theodore. He got up from the table and turned on the light. "Felicity, tell us straight out: What, if anything, do you know about ghosts?"

"Well, I read a book about them once," Felicity said, pulling the candle toward her and hugging it like a cup of tea. "I read that when a great tragedy has taken place somewhere, the feelings are so strong that they leave a psychic imprint in the atmosphere."

"Sort of like the image on the negative of a photograph?" Joseph suggested.

"Exactly. And the book said that whenever a person of unusual sensitivity comes upon the place where this tragedy occurred, he might see the scene as clearly as if he were there when it happened. Or, if not the scene, the ghost of a person to whom the great tragedy happened."

"But we have lived in this hotel now for over a year!" said Mother. "Why are we seeing a tragedy now?"

"What tragedy?" asked Delores. "All I see is this ghost standing at the foot of my bed."

"And with all due respect and love for my darling daughter, Delores," said Theodore, "I would consider her to be one of the least sensitive members of this family."

"Thanks a lot, Dad," Delores told him.

"There must be a reason why he appears in the same place every night," said Felicity. "It might just be, in fact, that Delores is in his room."

"*My* room," said Delores.

". . . And if you are sleeping in the ghost-boy's room—what used to be his room, that is—there is something he wants you to know."

"Well, Felicity," said Theodore, beginning to smile. "I have the perfect solution. Since you know so much about ghosts and Delores knows so little, and Delores needs her sleep so that she can become the Worker of the Week at the parachute factory, why don't you girls change places for a few nights? You can find out what the ghost has to tell us, Delores can get her sleep, and perhaps we will, at last, have some peace and quiet in this hotel."

"Oh, but I couldn't possibly," Felicity said. "At the moment, Mr. Magruder, I am in daily contact with a dead uncle who is buried on one side of the cemetery, and with my aunt, his dear departed wife, who is buried on the other. They didn't get on well at all, you see. Now that they are both dead, of course, they think perhaps they would like to be buried together after all, and the argument is which of them shall be dug up to be reburied beside whom. It is almost more than my poor head can stand."

"I see, I see," said Theodore, who didn't see at all.

"Well, we certainly don't want to tire you out," Mother said hastily. "Do go back to bed, dear Felicity, and this family will work out its problems alone, just as we have before. In fact, at this very moment, I can hear Mr. Lamkin breathing just beyond the door. It wouldn't surprise me in the least if Mrs. Buzzwell were with him and had been listening to everything we said."

"I have not!" came Mrs. Buzzwell's voice. "I came only because I heard Felicity getting up in the room above me and I just wanted to be sure she was all right." Mrs. Buzzwell peeped sheepishly from around old Mr. Lamkin, who had moved on into the apartment now, cupping one hand to his ear so as not to miss a single word.

Father sent them all back to bed—Felicity, Mrs. Buzzwell, and Mr. Lamkin, the hotel regulars. Then Delores moved in with Mother, Mr. Magruder squeezed in bed with Joseph, and Delores's room went empty for the rest of the night.

The next evening, however, as Mother feared, the newspaper put out a late edition that read in large letters across the top: BESSLEDORF GHOST BAFFLES HOTEL. People who had never so much as bought a cup of coffee in the hotel dining room were lining up out on the sidewalk for dinner, wanting to see the place the ghost had appeared.

And just as Theodore Magruder could have predicted, the news somehow reached Indianapolis, where Mr. Fairchild, the owner, lived. The phone rang as if on cue.

Bernie, who was helping out at the registration desk, looked at his dad. "Shall I get it?" he asked.

"We both know who it is," said Theodore. "No, I shall answer like a man." He picked up the receiver. "Bessledorf Hotel, the manager speaking," he said.

"Magruder, what the devil is going on in my hotel *this* time?" Fairchild yelled. Bernie could hear every word the man said.

"Well, it's not the devil, sir," said Mr. Magruder. "It appears to be the ghost of a young boy about Bernie's age, who has been appearing nightly in Delores's room and keeping us all awake."

"So what are you going to do about it?" Mr. Fairchild bellowed.

"Do, sir? We're simply doubling up in the other bedrooms the best we can."

"Is that all?"

"What would you suggest, sir? An exterminator?"

"Listen here, Magruder," came Mr. Fairchild's voice. Theodore held the receiver away from his head and rubbed his ear. "If that danged ghost has already made the newspaper down there in Middleburg, I'll bet you've got people already lined up on the sidewalk waiting to have a look."

"As a matter of fact . . ." Theodore began, but just at that moment the doors to the lobby opened and in walked Lester, carrying a lighted candle and followed by a crowd of people.

"I hear voices, Magruder," yelled Mr. Fairchild. "What's going on?"

"It . . . it appears, sir, that our youngest boy, Lester, is leading a tour."

"A tour, eh? And how much is he charging?"

Bernie noticed a sign around Lester's neck that read GHOST TOUR, TEN CENTS. "A dime," he told his father.

"A dime," Theodore repeated into the telephone.

"A *dime?*" roared Mr. Fairchild. "Magruder, I want you to play it up. I want a big sign out on the hotel canopy that says HOME OF THE BESSLEDORF GHOST, TOURS NIGHTLY. Every old hotel should have a ghost, you know."

"What . . . what do you want us to charge, sir?" asked Bernie's father.

"One dollar," said Mr. Fairchild. "Children, fifty cents."

5

Children, Fifty Cents

The sign went up on the hotel canopy the next day.

"Never saw such goings-on in my life," grumbled Wilbur Wilkins, the handyman, as he tacked it up. "Workin' for this hotel is one step removed from the loony bin, and that's the truth."

"Theodore," said Mother, "I will not have this! I will not have perfect strangers walking through our apartment every night, checking for dust on the dresser tops and looking in my closets."

"I assure you, my dear, that no one is interested in dust balls. What people want to see is the ghost."

"Well, they won't unless they come about three in the morning," Joseph reminded them.

"In which case," said Mother, "I shall pack my bags and leave."

"Now, Alma," said her husband, "even Mr. Fairchild is reasonable. No one expects us to let strangers into our bedrooms in the dead of night. It is quite sufficient to have an evening tour at nine o'clock."

"But what on earth will we show them for their dollar?" asked Delores.

"I suggest," said Bernie's father, "that the tour begin in the lobby. We will give our customers a brief history of the Bessledorf Hotel, then take them up the stairs to the second floor, down the corridor to the stairs leading to third, along the third floor to the elevator at the end, and then back to the lobby again. At this point every guest will be given a candle, and when the candles are lit, the lights will be extinguished, and slowly the procession will move into the hallway of our apartment, and on into Delores's bedroom, where the ghost has been seen."

Goose bumps rose up on Bernie's arms as he listened. "But . . ." he said, "what if all these people drive the ghost away and he never comes back?"

"So?" Delores snapped. "Isn't that exactly what we want to happen? If the ghost wanted to appear in our broom closet in the middle of the night, that's one thing, but not, by golly, at the foot of my bed."

Bernie just wasn't sure yet *how* he felt about the ghost. A little scared and a little curious, he guessed.

"I am now going to sit down at my desk and write the brief history of the hotel that I will tell our customers," Theodore said, checking his watch. "I do not wish to be disturbed for the next hour, Alma, and if anyone asks, the first tour takes place this evening."

The problem was that there had to be several helpers for each tour, Mother insisted, to keep the customers from wandering into the other rooms and looking in the apartment kitchen to see if the Magruders had done their dishes. If Father was the tour guide, she would have to be at the front desk while he was taking the customers around. And Delores, who worked full-time at the parachute factory sewing straps and pounding grommets, and Joseph, who went to veterinary school, were always tired when they got home at night. They could hardly be expected to help out on the tours as well. That left only Bernie and Lester, and if the crowd were large, even they would have trouble controlling it.

"Can I ask Georgene and Weasel if they want to help out, too?" Bernie asked his father.

"Absolutely," said Theodore. "For ten percent of the ticket price. If only one person shows up for a tour, you get ten cents. If twenty people show up, you get two dollars to divide among you."

Bernie began to think that this must be the most exciting thing that had ever happened at the Bessledorf Hotel since his father became manager. And there had been a lot of exciting things happen—a Mad Gasser on the loose, bodies that kept appearing, then disappearing, in the rooms . . . ! This time, however, Bernie and his friends had a job, and he couldn't wait to tell the others.

At lunchtime, the four of them, including Lester, sat out on the wall by the alley and discussed what they should wear.

"I think we should wear white shirts and blue pants, just like the ushers in a theater," said Georgene.

"Something better than that," said Weasel. "What about black top hats?"

"And black capes," added Bernie.

"And black boots!" said Lester.

"How about the lot of you putting paper bags over your head and walking right into the river?" said Officer Feeney, who was cutting through the alley on his daily rounds. "Biggest bunch of foolishness I ever heard. You wouldn't know a ghost if it sat in your lap."

"It was you who told me about feeling a cold draft when a ghost was around, Feeney," Bernie told him. "And that's just what it's like when he comes to the foot of Delores's bed."

"That so?" said Feeney. "Cold like the wind?"

Bernie nodded.

"Like snow?"

"Like ice," said Bernie.

"Hmmm," said Feeney, frowning just a bit. "Don't like the sound of that. It's a bit of a mystery, all right." And he went on down the alley saying, "Hmmm."

"About our uniforms . . ." said Georgene again.

"There are some old hotel uniforms up in the storage attic," Bernie said. "Let's look there."

The storage room was reached by a pull-chain stairway in the ceiling of the third-floor hallway. Bernie pulled it down, and they all climbed up. It was dusty. The small attic room was hot. But in a wardrobe off to the side were some old doormen's uniforms, some cooks' uniforms, some aprons, hats, capes, boots, and waiters' jackets.

The four children tried them on and made their choices, even though the clothes were a little large. Georgene decided on white Levi's and one of the waiter's white jackets; Bernie and Weasel picked deep blue doormen's capes with gold braid on the shoulders; and Lester chose boots a little too large for him and a chauffeur's cap that slid down his forehead and almost covered his eyes.

At twenty minutes of nine that evening, there were a dozen people gathered in the hotel lobby, waiting for the tour to begin. By five minutes to nine the crowd had grown to thirty or more. Mixed Blessing walked about, sniffing the shoes of the customers; Lewis and Clark observed the people from the top of the sofa;

and Salt Water kept them all entertained with his rau-
cous "Shake a leg!" and "Hiya, babe."

Bernie appeared with his brother and his friends, all
of them looking very sharp indeed in their uniforms.
And when the big grandfather clock in the corner
struck nine, the door of the apartment opened and out
stepped Theodore. He was wearing the dark navy blue
suit that he usually wore to funerals, and was looking
very somber. A hush fell over the lobby as the guests
turned expectantly in his direction.

"Shake a leg!" squealed Salt Water. A few people
laughed. Bernie threw the cover over Salt Water's
cage. And Salt Water, being stupid, thought it was
nighttime already, and promptly went to sleep.

"Ladies and gentlemen," said Theodore, his hands
folded in front of him. "You are here because you have
heard of the unusual happenings that have been going
on in our famed hotel."

Bernie listened proudly. Theodore had a grand,
deep voice that rang like bells when he spoke. In fact,
this was the first time that Bernie had ever heard that
the Bessledorf Hotel was famous.

"It is not surprising, however, that a ghost should
honor us with his presence, because the Bessledorf is
over one hundred twenty-five years old. Who knows
what celebrations and tragedies have taken place in its
rooms? Who knows what famous personages have slept

in its beds? Who knows what stories the walls could tell us, or what secrets the very floorboards beneath you could whisper? Who knows . . . ?"

"Who *does*?" somebody called out. "Let's get on with the tour, Magruder! We want to see the ghost."

"Yes, yes!" people yelled. And then they began to chant: "We want the ghost! We want the ghost!"

Bernie knew that the crowd had begun to lose patience with his father. All Theodore seemed to be giving them was questions that were never answered.

"Please!" said Theodore. "Ladies and gentlemen, please! I can't promise that you will see the ghost. What I have promised you is a tour of the hotel, including the room where the ghost appears. Whether or not he will choose to appear while you are here is entirely up to him, but I assure you that each and every one of you will be taken inside the room, to the very spot where this strange apparition makes his appearance."

"How much?" someone asked.

"Adults, one dollar; children, fifty cents."

Finally the money was collected, and with Bernie, Georgene, Weasel, and Lester bringing up the rear, the crowd moved through the lobby and up the stairs to the second floor.

Unfortunately, Theodore's speech continued on the second floor.

"Who knows what murders may have taken place behind these closed doors? Who knows . . . ?"

"Who cares?" yelled somebody else. "On with the bloody tour!"

By the time the group reached the third floor, Theodore was running out of things to say. People crowded into the elevator, six or seven at a time, and Bernie pushed the button sending them back to the lobby. There each guest was given a candle; Georgene helped light them. The overhead lights were turned out and the crowd hushed. With Mr. Magruder leading the way, the tour moved back behind the registration desk and through the door leading to the Magruders' apartment.

Mother had strung ribbon across the doors where she did not want people to go. The crowd moved quietly along the hallway and into Delores's bedroom. There they stood in hushed silence along the wall, staring at the flickering candle at the foot of her bed.

"Here in this room," intoned Theodore, "about a week ago, at the hour of two in the morning, my darling daughter, Delores, was awakened from her slumbers by a cold draft of air, the icy realization that some ethereal creature was afoot on this very floor where you are standing now. 'Who's there?' she cried, but the only answer she got was the sound of the wind banging the shutters."

"What shutters?" Georgene whispered to Bernie.

He shrugged. "We'll get some," he told her.

"And then," Theodore continued, "into the bedroom came this column of light, as dim as the moon's halo, and as Delores stared, the misty figure of a boy made his appearance."

"What did the ghost say?" somebody asked.

"Not a word," said Theodore.

"What did the ghost do?" asked a woman.

"It raised its arms like this," said Theodore, slowly raising his arms over his head.

"And then . . . ?" asked a man in one corner.

"Then . . ." said Theodore, "it vanished, just as it had come, growing fainter and fainter until at last there was nothing."

"What happened next?" asked a big woman in a gray dress.

Mr. Magruder began talking rapidly again, aware that the climax was over, desperately trying to keep the attention of the crowd. "Then Delores, my only daughter, rushed from her bed, a wild scream of terror in her throat, and collapsed here in the hallway, where we found her."

Bernie hadn't remembered it quite that way, but it did make a good story. For several minutes the crowd stood very still, looking and listening, hoping that the ghost would come.

"Well, I'm not going to wait all night," a man said at last.

People were disappointed, Bernie could tell. But they contented themselves with standing in the exact place the ghost had stood and touching the candle that flickered at the foot of Delores's bed. Some even wanted their pictures taken there in the room, husbands and wives together, and Theodore had to snap the camera. By this time others were wandering off, wanting to peek in the rest of the bedrooms, and it took Bernie, Lester, Georgene, Weasel, and even Mixed Blessing to keep them moving in a steady line until they were all outside again.

"If this doesn't take the cake!" said Officer Feeney, who was standing out on the sidewalk. "I could tell you I saw the ghost of a dead boy sittin' behind the wheel of my Buick and charge a dollar to let folks have a peek in my car. There's a sucker born every minute, that's for certain."

Bernie, however, knew that this wasn't a gyp. There *had* been a ghost. He believed it, and while his father might stretch the truth a bit to make a good story, he would never make up a lie.

"Wow!" said Weasel when the last guest had gone. "This was fun, and we're going to get paid for it! My first summer job!"

"As long as people keep coming, you have a job," Theodore promised.

The next day, however, as Bernie, Lester, Georgene, and Weasel sat on the curb in front of the hotel,
eating cherries and seeing how far they could spit the
seeds, Bernie said, "I think we need to find out more
about the history of the hotel. I don't think the customers found Dad's talk very interesting. If *I* paid a
dollar to go on the tour, I'd want to know more about
the people who used to live here."

"How are we going to do that?" said Weasel.

"We could go to the courthouse or the library,"
Bernie said. "Maybe someone there could show us
where to look."

"That could take weeks!" said Georgene. "The
ghost could be gone by then."

"I hope not," said Bernie, then wondered why he'd
said it. Didn't they all want the ghost to go so Delores
could have her bedroom back? Wasn't that the point?

After his friends had gone home and Bernie was
waiting in the lobby for his mother to get dinner, he
thought again about going to the library to look up
everything he could find on the history of the Bessledorf. It wasn't the hotel so much that he wanted to
know about, however. It was the ghost.

6

Library Lock-in

The next morning Bernie, Georgene, and Weasel went to the library to see if there were any books about their town—books that just might say something about the Bessledorf Hotel.

They looked in the computer listing of topics until they came to the M's. "Middleburg," the computer read. "Middleburg, Indiana, History of . . ." Georgene copied down the reference numbers of the books listed, and they went to the shelf. Weasel ran his finger along the numbers of all the books in the row, but *Middleburg, Past and Present*, the book they most wanted to see, was missing. They went to the librarian.

"I'll bet Mrs. Hamilton has it," she told them, and motioned toward a thin woman who was seated at a library table surrounded by books, papers, and maps. "Mrs. Hamilton is writing a book about the history of Middleburg's gardens, and every day she comes to the library and takes a stack of books to the table with her."

The three children walked quietly over to the table where Mrs. Hamilton was working. With her right hand she was scribbling furiously. With her left she was looking things up in books. *From Asters to Zinnias*, read the title of one book. *The Cultivation of Poppies*, read another. *Middleburg, Past and Present* was lying to one side. Just as Bernie was getting up his nerve to ask if they might borrow it for a while, Mrs. Hamilton grabbed the book, opened it to a certain page, and scribbled some more in her notes.

Bernie, Georgene, and Weasel waited politely. They walked around the library and looked at all the maps on the walls. They went into the children's section to see if there were any new books by Beverly Cleary or Larry Callen. They took turns at the drinking fountain and studied the Indian arrowheads in a glass case by the front door. But when they came back to the table where Mrs. Hamilton was sitting, she was still hard at work, holding the book that Bernie wanted.

"I've got to go take my trombone lesson," said Weasel.

"And I've got to vacuum the upstairs for Mother," said Georgene. "I promised I'd do it today."

"It's okay," said Bernie. "I'll stick around. She's got to go to lunch sometime. I'll get the book then."

Twelve o'clock came, and one of the librarians went to lunch. A lot of people who had been studying and reading at other tables got up and went home. But not Mrs. Hamilton. Twelve-thirty came, and finally one o'clock.

Mrs. Hamilton put down her pen. She reached for her purse and set it on her lap. She was still holding *Middleburg, Past and Present* in her left hand, but with her right she opened her purse and reached down inside. Out came a gumdrop, which she popped into her mouth. Then another and another. She scribbled some more. She ate some more.

"Excuse me," said Bernie finally, "but could I . . . ?"

"Shhh," Mrs. Hamilton said sternly. Bernie gave up and went home.

At four o'clock, however, he went back to the library. It closed at six, and surely Mrs. Hamilton was through by now. He couldn't believe it. She was still in exactly the same chair at the same table, and in her left hand, she still held the library's only copy of *Mid-*

dleburg, Past and Present. Bernie went to talk to the librarian.

"Mrs. Hamilton comes here every day," the librarian said. "When I get here in the morning, she is already waiting at the door, and she is the last one to leave at night."

"Can I wait until she puts the book back on the shelf at six o'clock and then check it out for the night?" Bernie asked.

"I'm afraid not," the librarian said. "That's a reference book, and they have to be used here."

"Could you ask her if I could borrow it for a little while?" Bernie suggested.

"Let's put it this way," the librarian told him. "This book she is writing is the most important thing in the world to her. Mrs. Hamilton is head of the Middleburg Garden Club and the Democratic Women's Society; she is the wife of the president of the First National Bank of Middleburg, and her brother is on the library board. If you were in my shoes, would *you* ask her?"

Bernie shook his head and walked away. There was only one thing he could think of to do. At ten minutes to six, when the lights began to blink to remind people that the library was closing, Bernie went into the supply closet and hid behind the vacuum cleaner. He knew that the janitor came early in the morning to clean, not in the evening, so he hoped that no one would check the closet before the library closed.

He heard the bell ring at five minutes to six. He heard footsteps as people went out the door. He heard the librarians saying goodnight to each other as they got out their car keys. And he heard the front door clang shut.

At last there were no sounds at all in the library. Bernie waited another five minutes just to be sure. Then slowly he opened the closet door and stepped out. The lights were off, and everyone was gone.

He went back to the reference book shelf, and there it was—*Middleburg, Past and Present.* It smelled vaguely like gumdrops, but he didn't care. He sat down and looked through the index at the back. "Bessledorf Bus Station, Bessledorf Cat Clinic, Bessledorf Dry Cleaners, Bessledorf Funeral Home, Bessledorf Hotel . . ." Bernie turned to page seventy-two and began reading.

> The Bessledorf Hotel is located halfway up the hill at the west end of Bessledorf Street. Originally the home of Colonel Horace Bessledorf, for whom the street was named, it was first known as the Bessledorf Mansion, and contained twelve bedrooms, a winter kitchen, a summer kitchen, a

library, a formal dining room, a parlor, a ballroom, and a grand staircase. In addition, there was a porch that extended around three sides of the house as well as numerous outbuildings, a machine shed, and a stable.

Bernie tried to imagine what the building looked like when it had been a house. He read on about the big sloping lawn in back that led to the river, and could almost see ladies in long skirts and men in tall hats walking grandly about on the grass. He hurriedly read some more:

Colonel Horace Bessledorf built the magnificent home in 1864 for his wife Amanda and their six children: Percy, 15; Thomas, 14; Elizabeth, 11; Spencer, 8; Clara, 5, and Jonathan, only 1. In 1865 a great fire, caused by lightning, destroyed much of the third floor, but the house was rebuilt that same year. In 1866, however, the Colonel was killed by a fall from a horse. His widow had scarcely begun to deal with her grief when Elizabeth, her older daughter, died of diphtheria. In 1874, when Jonathan, her youngest child, was killed in a fall down the grand staircase, Mrs. Bessledorf's grief was so great, it is said, that she held her dead child in her arms all night and insisted on burying him herself. The following year relatives prevailed upon the family to leave the scene of so many tragedies and move to Michigan. The Bessledorf mansion was sold to a furniture manufacturer, then to a lawyer, and finally, in 1925, it was renovated into a thirty-room hotel, called the Bessledorf. The grand ballroom became the present lobby and dining room, and the summer porch and kitchen behind the building became an apartment for a succession of hotel managers and their families. The front porch was removed, and all that remains today of the original mansion is a portion of the grand staircase, now only half as wide, which can be seen to your left as you enter the lobby. It is said that the last word spoken by Amanda Bessledorf upon her own death in 1919 was simply, "Jonathan."

"Wow!" said Bernie. Wait till he told Georgene and Weasel! Wait till *Father* heard, in fact! Now they would *really* have something to tell on their tours through the hotel!

If, as he thought, the ghost was someone who had died in the hotel—a boy his own age, that someone would have to have been . . . Bernie read the paragraph again. Jonathan Bessledorf was only a year old in 1864 and he died in 1874. Goose bumps rose up all over Bernie's body. Jonathan Bessledorf was eleven years old when he died!

He took the book over to a copier, put a dime in the slot, and made a copy of the page about the Bessledorf Hotel. Then he carefully put the book back on the shelf in exactly the same place he got it, and went to the door. The door was locked.

Bernie had expected the door to be locked from the outside, of course, but he had thought it would still open from the inside. He tried the back door that led to an alley. The back door was locked. He tried the side door beside the ramp where books were delivered. The side door was locked as well. The windows were locked. *Everything* was locked. Bernie Magruder was locked in for the night, and at this very moment, his family, he knew, was sitting down to dinner. He went to the phone at the reception desk and called home. The line was busy.

He waited a few minutes and tried again. Still busy. He knew his parents were probably calling all over the neighborhood, wondering where he was. The later it got, the more worried they would be. Finally he dialed Weasel's number.

"Bernie, where are you?" Weasel said. "Your dad just called here and wondered where you were."

"Listen, Weasel, I'm locked in the library. I hid in the closet so I could read the book about Middleburg after Mrs. Hamilton went home, and now I can't get out."

There was only one thing to do, and Bernie knew what it was.

"I'll get Officer Feeney," said Weasel.

It seemed like an hour to Bernie before anyone came, but finally he heard the sound of a car pulling up outside, footsteps on the concrete, then the voices of Officer Feeney and Weasel as a key turned in the lock.

"What the ding-dong have we got here?" asked the policeman, throwing open the door. "A boy that hasn't got sense enough to find his way out of the library at closing time?"

"I was interested in a book," said Bernie.

"And you didn't hear the folks going home? Didn't see the lights turning off?" Feeney waited until Bernie was out on the steps, then locked the door again behind him. "The vice squad I could have had! Robbery detail I could have had! Auto theft, even! And what do I get? A downtown beat with the Magruders on my block—candlelight ghost tours through an old hotel and a boy locked up in the library. You better get yourself home, Bernie, before your pa warms the seat of your pants."

"Thanks, Feeney," Bernie told him, as he and Weasel ran off down the sidewalk.

"What did you find out?" Weasel asked, holding onto his glasses as they ran.

"I got the book and copied a page!" Bernie said breathlessly. "And I think I know who the ghost is. Or was."

"Who?"

"Jonathan Bessledorf. He was eleven years old when he died falling down the grand staircase."

"*What* grand staircase?"

"The stairs leading down from the second floor. They used to be twice as wide as they are now, and they led all the way to the ballroom."

"*What* ballroom?"

"The lobby. It used to be a ballroom with a grand staircase, and Jonathan fell down the stairs and his mother buried him herself."

"Where?"

"The cemetery, where else?" said Bernie. "We'll go over there tomorrow and find his grave."

Bernie's mother had his dinner saved for him on the stove, and she was just going to take her place in the hotel restaurant, where she showed customers to their tables, when Bernie walked in.

"Bernie, where on earth . . . ?" she said, worriedly.

"I was locked in the library, Mom, but it was worth it," he said.

"What?"

"I'll tell you later," he promised.

There were so many things on his mind that he could hardly keep them all in. Would the ghost come back to Delores's bedroom? And what would happen if, some night, Bernie was waiting there when it did? And what would happen if, when the ghost appeared, Bernie said, "Jonathan, is that you?"

7

Something Missing

Theodore Magruder was delighted to see what Bernie had found at the library. That very evening, in his guided tour through the Bessledorf Hotel, he pointed out what used to be the grand staircase that a child had fallen down to his death, the lobby and hotel dining room, which had once been the grand ballroom, and he told how, after all the tragic happenings in Colonel Horace Bessledorf's family, relatives moved the grieving widow to Michigan. It made the tour much more interesting.

"Nice going, Bernie!" Theodore told him. "Nice going, indeed!"

But Mrs. Magruder was uneasy.

"I don't like this, Theodore," she said the next

morning. "It's the same thing happening all over again. Just after Colonel Bessledorf had completed his magnificent house, bad things started to happen. And right after we mended the roof, put a new floor in the cellar, and replaced a broken window, what do we get but a ghost? If I woke up someday to find one of our own dear children missing, I should never forgive myself for staying in this strange place."

"My dear, dear Alma," said Bernie's father, "how can you say such a thing? You love the Bessledorf as much as I, and you know it. We are the managers of a thriving hotel, with live entertainment in the dining room on weekends, and more and more guests filling our rooms each night. This is our home, our refuge, our castle, our escape from a troubled world. Here our children are safe."

"Yeah, Mom," said Bernie. "It's home, all right."

Bernie did not want to leave Middleburg no matter what—even if there were ten ghosts in the hotel. The family had traveled from one place to another like dry leaves on a windy day, and now that Mr. Magruder liked his job at the hotel, Bernie wanted to stay. At the same time, of course, he didn't exactly like the thought of waking up some morning missing.

Lester was making a peanut-butter-and-banana milkshake in the kitchen blender.

"Who do you think the ghost will take, Bernie?" he asked, pouring his drink into a glass and then licking the rim of the blender. He ran his fingers along the inside of the container and licked those, too. Bernie tried not to watch.

"I bet it'll be you," Lester said. "How come you figure the ghost wants you, Bernie?"

"Who says it'll be me?" Bernie said irritably, and went outside.

When Georgene and Weasel came over, he asked them to go with him to the cemetery. "If we can find Jonathan's grave," he said, "it might tell us a *little* bit more about him."

"Assuming that the ghost is really Jonathan Bessledorf," said Georgene.

The cemetery was on the other side of Middleburg Park, down near the Middleburg River. It was a hot, dusty walk, and the sun was fierce. When they reached the gates of the cemetery, they collapsed in the shade of a hickory tree until they caught their breath.

"Maybe someone pushed him," said Weasel at last, sprawled out on the grass.

"Who?" asked Bernie.

"Jonathan. How do you kill yourself falling down the stairs?"

"Easy," said Georgene. "You break your neck. Have you noticed how steep those stairs are between the lobby and the second floor? Imagine Jonathan standing at the very top and tripping or something."

"Maybe one of his brothers pushed him," said Weasel, squinting at the sky through his glasses. "Maybe he's come back to push somebody else just to get even. Bernie, for instance."

"How would *that* make it even?" Georgene wanted to know. "Bernie never even *knew* Jonathan Bessledorf."

"Don't ask me, ask the ghost," said Weasel. "I'm only telling you what I think."

Bernie got up suddenly. Every time anyone talked about the ghost, they just assumed it had come for him. "Let's go find the grave," he said.

The three friends had been to the cemetery before, but they had never paid much attention to the gravestones. If the Bessledorf family was so rich that a whole street was named after them, Bernie figured that the family plot in the cemetery would be especially grand, so he looked for the tallest gravestone there. They walked over to some marble monuments in the center of the cemetery, and there they were, the Bessledorf graves, surrounded by a low brick wall.

First there was the grand tombstone for Colonel Horace Bessledorf. There was a sculpture of a man on the top of it, riding a horse. The engraved letters read:

COLONEL HORACE BESSLEDORF,
BORN 1829, DIED 1866. BELOVED HUSBAND
OF AMANDA AND FATHER OF

PERCY, THOMAS, ELIZABETH,
SPENCER, CLARA, AND JONATHAN. GONE
BUT NOT FORGOTTEN.

"Wow!" said Weasel respectfully as they stepped gently across the grass to the next grave.

ELIZABETH MYRTLE BESSLEDORF, read the next gravestone, with an engraving of a little angel holding a lamb:

HER LIFE ON EARTH WAS BLISSF'LY SPENT,
TILL GOD IN HEAVEN FOR HER SENT.

"That's a lousy poem," said Weasel.

"Shhh," said Georgene, and moved on to the next grave in line. But it was not the grave of Jonathan Bessledorf, it was the grave of Colonel Bessledorf's cousin, and next to that his aunt. There were no graves of Mrs. Bessledorf nor any of the remaining children. Jonathan was missing.

"It doesn't make sense," said Georgene. "I can see why the mother and the other children would be buried somewhere else after they moved to Michigan, but Jonathan died here in Middleburg."

"Did the book in the library actually say that Jonathan was buried in Middleburg Cemetery?" Weasel asked.

"No," said Bernie. "It just said that his mother buried him herself."

"Then he's probably in your backyard," said Weasel.

"*What* backyard?" asked Bernie. "It's cement right out to the alley."

"Well, I'll bet he's under a lilac bush at the side, then," said Georgene. "Mothers always bury their children under lilac bushes or rosebushes or something."

Was it possible? Bernie wondered. They went back home and spent the rest of the morning looking around the bushes at both sides of the hotel, but there was no gravestone. Maybe Jonathan was buried *without* a marker, in which case he could be anywhere—under the alley, even, before it was an alley, of course— when the backyard was a long, sloping lawn leading down to the river. But somehow it just didn't seem likely that a mother would bury her child without any gravestone at all.

When Georgene and Weasel went home for lunch, Bernie wandered over to the courthouse and asked the clerk how to find the death certificate of someone who died in 1874.

"Just tell me the name, and I'll look it up for you," the clerk said. Bernie told him. The clerk put the name on a computer and let Bernie watch as the names flashed on a screen.

"There it is," said the clerk. "Jonathan Alfred Bessledorf. Born 1863, died 1874. Cause of death: skull fracture, accidental fall."

"Does it say where he was buried?" Bernie asked.

"Nope," said the clerk. "They don't put that on death certificates. But you might try the churches. Sometimes they keep records."

Bernie was beginning to feel very good at detective work. He was finding out a lot about the Bessledorf family that Theodore, with all his duties at the hotel, simply did not have time to look for. Now he had to figure out which church the Bessledorfs attended when they lived in Middleburg, over a hundred years ago, and he wondered how he could possibly do that.

There were only three churches downtown—the First Baptist, the Good Shepherd Lutheran, and Saint Paul's Catholic Church at the end of the street. Bernie hoped that, since there were no automobiles in the 1870s, the Bessledorfs would have chosen a church near their house. He walked to the First Baptist up near the parachute factory and looked for the cornerstone that told when the building was built. There it was, plain as day: 1901. It couldn't have been First Baptist.

Bernie went down the street in the other direction to the Catholic church. This was an older church, and it was more difficult to find the cornerstone, but finally there it was, behind a bank of weeds. It read 1895. It wasn't Saint Paul's either.

The Good Shepherd Lutheran was across town in still another direction. There were so many bushes around the base of the building that Bernie didn't see how he could possibly find the cornerstone. He had to crawl on his hands and knees, pushing back brambles. But at last he discovered it. "Built 1860," he read. Aha!

"May I help you, young man?" said a voice behind him, and Bernie almost fell over. Slowly he untangled himself from the branches and stood up to face the minister, who was out for his afternoon stroll.

"I was just trying to find out when your church was built," Bernie said sheepishly.

"Ah! Interested in churches, are you? Wonderful old building, isn't it? Look at those stained-glass windows up there. Imported from Italy, that's what they are. The pews were made in France and shipped over, and the . . ."

"I just wanted to know where somebody was buried," Bernie broke in, afraid that the minister might be building up to a sermon.

"Well, that's one thing we don't have, a graveyard," the minister said. "All we do is preach the funeral service."

"Would you have a record of the funeral, then?"

"All the way back to when the church began," the minister said. "What would you like to know?"

Bernie followed him into the study and asked him about a funeral service for Jonathan Bessledorf in 1874. He sat on a cushioned chair and waited while the minister got out an old leather book that was so yellow with age that the edges of the pages had begun to crumble. He turned them gently until he came to the year 1874.

" 'Jonathan Alfred Bessledorf, age 11,' " he read aloud. " 'On the twentieth day of June 1874, Amanda Bessledorf and her four surviving children, with relatives in attendance, gathered in the church chapel to mourn the untimely death of her youngest son, who was killed accidentally in a fall down the stairs. The service, being somewhat unusual in that the deceased had already been buried at home by his mother, was deemed sufficient for a Christian burial, in that the body had already been examined by a doctor and an official pronouncement made. Prayers were offered for the soul of the deceased child and for the consolation of the distraught widow, who collapsed during the service and had to be supported by her kin. She was helped into a carriage at the conclusion of the service and driven back to the house where so many tragedies had occurred.' "

"People can just be buried right in their own yards?" Bernie asked the minister.

"Back then they could, I guess. Does seem a bit strange, doesn't it? You're thinking this has something to do with that ghost I've been reading about in the newspaper?"

"I don't know," said Bernie. "I can't help wondering."

He walked home very slowly. Most of Colonel Bessledorf's land had been divided up over the years and sold long ago—to the funeral parlor, the bus depot, the dry cleaners, the pet store. Jonathan's body could be buried deep in the ground under any one of those buildings. And, anyway, did it really matter? Bernie wasn't even sure it did. But one thing was becoming more clear: If he was going to find out why the ghost had come in the first place and why he kept returning, Bernie was going to have to ask the ghost himself.

He shivered despite the warmth of the afternoon. This time the goose bumps stayed with him all the way home.

8

The Light
on the Stairs

Bernie was very quiet at the dinner table that night.

"You haven't touched your mashed potatoes," said his mother. "Are you ill, Bernie?"

"No, just thinking," he said.

"Well, *I'm* ill!" Delores murmured. "I am sick to death of not being able to sleep in my own bedroom because of an eleven-year-old ghost, and terrified when I try. I tried to sleep in there again last night, Dad, and back he came. I knocked over a chair getting out. I think we should hire someone to get rid of him."

"Get *rid* of him?" Bernie gasped, as though enough bad things hadn't happened to Jonathan Bessledorf already. He was almost beginning to like the boy.

"Get rid of him?" echoed Father. "Delores, my girl, do you realize that every night the tours are a little larger than they were the night before? The hotel is earning quite a bit of money from the ghost tours, and Mr. Fairchild has promised that when we have taken in a thousand dollars, he will replace our banisters and put a new rug in the parlor. The Bessledorf Hotel will look absolutely grand, and I will be manager of the finest hotel in Middleburg."

"I'd rather have my room back," said Delores.

"I'd rather have our *apartment* back," snapped Mother. "I am sick of tourists traipsing down our hallway every evening. Yesterday, when I was revising *Quivering Lips*, I could feel one of them breathing over my shoulder to see what I was writing. We have no privacy whatever."

"I don't know," said Lester. "I sort of like it. All my friends think it's cool. I agree with Bernie. I don't want to drive the ghost away."

"That's easy for *you* to say," said Delores. "It's not *your* bedroom he's haunting."

Joseph had been very quiet at the table, and finally Mr. Magruder turned to him. "What do *you* think we should do, Joseph?" he asked.

"Well, I was thinking," said Joseph, "that animals are usually very quick to sense when a stranger intends to do you harm. But now that the ghost has come a few times, our pets aren't that upset by him anymore. It's almost as though they feel he belongs here."

"He does," said Bernie. "He's Jonathan Bessledorf."

"We don't know that for sure," said Mother.

"He was eleven years old when he died," Bernie told them. "I checked out his death certificate at the courthouse. And then I found a record of his funeral service at the Good Shepherd Lutheran Church."

"We already knew when he died from that book you read in the library," said Father.

"But we don't know where the body is buried," Bernie told him.

Everyone stopped chewing and looked down the table at Bernie. Delores turned pale.

"If there's a record of a funeral service, surely it mentioned where the burial took place," Mother ventured.

"That's just the point," Bernie told her. "All the records show is that Jonathan fell down the stairs and fractured his skull, and that after he died, his mother held him in her arms all night long before she buried him herself. But it doesn't say exactly *where*. He's not in Middleburg Cemetery with the other Bessledorfs; I've checked. The record of the funeral service says that the mother buried Jonathan at home. Weasel and

Georgene think he's probably under a rosebush or something."

Delores looked at the vase of fresh roses in the center of the table that Mother had cut from the bushes at the side of the hotel.

"I shall never pick another flower as long as I live," she said.

"Delores, don't be daft," said her father. "Jonathan could be buried anywhere at all. The Bessledorf property ran all the way down to the river back then. The poor boy could be buried under the back alley, for all we know."

"Then why does he choose my room to walk in each night?" Delores said. "There must have been enough bedrooms on the second and third floors for all the Bessledorf children and their relatives as well."

"I don't know," said Theodore, "but let's find out. Bernie, I want you to get the heaviest blanket you can find in our closet, and all of you follow me out to the lobby."

Bernie got up from the table and quickly got a thick comforter that his parents used in winter. When he reached the lobby, the entire family was assembled as well as the dog, the cats, the parrot, and Felicity Jones. Old Mr. Lamkin and Mrs. Buzzwell played gin rummy in the corner.

"Now," said Father, "I want you to take that blanket to the top of the staircase, Bernie, and wrap yourself up in it."

The family looked at Theodore. Mr. Lamkin and Mrs. Buzzwell turned slowly around and stared.

Bernie walked up the steep staircase until he reached the door to the second floor, and wrapped the blanket around him.

"Now," said Father, "lie down, Bernie, and roll down the stairs."

"Theodore!" cried Mother. "One child has already died on those stairs. Do you want another?"

"It's quite all right, Alma. The blanket will protect him," Theodore said, and then to Bernie, "Let your body move of its own accord, and we shall see where it stops."

"I don't know why I continue to live here," said Mrs. Buzzwell. "Every day with the Magruders as managers is worse than the one before."

"Wheeee!" cried Mr. Lamkin delightedly. "This is better than a circus!"

With everyone watching, Bernie lay down, wrapped up inside the blanket like a hot dog in a bun, and rolled. *Thump, bumpity, bump, bump.* As he moved, he picked up speed, going faster and faster. Lewis and Clark scattered in two directions, Mixed Blessing barked, and Salt Water squawked. At the bottom of the stairs, Bernie rolled right out of the blanket and kept going until he came to a stop against the wall of the Magruder apartment. On the other side of the wall was Delores's bedroom.

At that moment the front door of the hotel opened and Officer Feeney, who had looked through the window, rushed in. "What happened?" he called. "Who fell?"

"It's only my brother," said Lester.

"Jumping Jehosephat! Shall I call an ambulance?" Feeney asked.

"We are acting out a death scene, Officer Feeney. Relax," said Bernie's father as Bernie sat up. "Do you know what I am thinking?" he asked his family. "If that wall had not been there, as it may not have been when this was the Bessledorf Mansion, Bernie would have rolled right to the spot where Delores's bedroom is now. That must be where Jonathan was when he died, where he was when he was found, and where it was that his dear sweet mother held him in her arms all night long. Perhaps that's why he comes to the foot of your bed, Delores."

"He wants me to hold him in my arms?" she shrieked.

"Perhaps he's just returning to the scene of his death," said Theodore.

"So pull up my rug," said Delores. "Maybe he's buried under my floorboards."

"Call the Ghostbusters," yelped old Mr. Lamkin. "I've seen 'em on TV."

"Ghosts are like mice," said Mrs. Buzzwell, her voice like gravel going down a tin chute. "If you don't get rid of the first one, you'll have them all over the place."

"I think we should leave a rose and a mirror at the foot of Delores's bed," said Felicity Jones. "The rose, so the ghost will know we love him, and the mirror so that when he looks in it, he will, perhaps, realize that he is dead."

"*I* think," said Theodore, "that we ought to be getting ready for our evening tour. If you will excuse us, Officer Feeney . . ."

"I think I'd rather be on homicide," said Feeney, and disappeared out the front door.

When the tour was over around nine-thirty, Theodore said, "Well, Alma, there's another twenty-seven dollars and fifty cents. This is turning out to be a very nice business. A few more weeks and we shall have enough for the new rug in the parlor. And you shall choose it yourself, any color you like."

"But this isn't a home anymore, Theodore," Mother said. "We are frightened, we have lost a bedroom, and I am tired of doubling up. If the ghost leaves of his own accord, that wouldn't be so bad, would it?"

"Of course not," said her husband. "But I do not

want Ghostbusters or any other kind of exterminators doing the job. Bernie is right. If this *is* the ghost of young Jonathan Bessledorf, he must have come for a reason."

About eleven o'clock, Bernie helped his father lock up. He put the cats in the cellar, threw the cover over the parrot's cage, and gave Mixed Blessing a dog yummy. Then he went to his bedroom and crawled in the bunk over Lester.

"Bernie," said Lester, "what do you suppose it feels like to be a ghost?"

"Sort of watery, I guess," Bernie told him.

"What do you suppose they do for fun?"

"If you ever fall down a grand staircase and fracture your skull, you'll find out, Lester," Bernie told him, and rolled over. He just didn't feel like talking; he didn't feel like doing anything except solving the mystery of Jonathan Bessledorf.

He could tell that Lester was asleep a while later because he heard him breathing, but Bernie wasn't tired. He got up about midnight for some crackers and milk in the kitchen, but when he came back to bed again, he still didn't feel like sleeping.

What was it like, he wondered, to be an eleven-year-old boy back in the 1870s, in a big house with a lawn that reached to the river, a father who had been killed when he fell off a horse, and a sister who had died of diphtheria? He wondered if Jonathan Bessledorf ever worried about what was going to happen to his family, as Bernie used to worry about his own—all the years when Father was working at first one job and then another.

The main thing, Bernie figured, is that you want to be remembered. If you have to die young, at least you don't want people to forget you. He wondered how Jonathan would have felt knowing that he wouldn't be there in the graveyard beside his father. When *he* died, Bernie decided, he wanted the tallest tombstone in the whole cemetery—a statue of Bernie on his skateboard, maybe, right there at the top, the first thing you could see when you walked in the cemetery.

He wasn't sure just what time it was—possibly two in the morning—when he heard Mixed Blessing give a soft, mournful howl. Bernie went out in the hallway, but he didn't see anything, didn't feel anything, so he opened the apartment door and went on out into the lobby and sat down on the sofa, the dog at his feet.

Suddenly the room seemed to be getting colder and colder and lighter and lighter. It couldn't be morning already, Bernie thought. He looked around. And then he saw it—a dim column of light at the very top of the staircase. Bernie's hand stopped scratching Mixed Blessing's ear. His heart, he felt sure, had stopped beating. The column of light grew brighter still, and finally the misty form of an eleven-year-old boy began moving slowly down the stairs.

Bernie had thought he wanted to talk to the ghost. He had thought he wanted to ask if his name was Jonathan, and what it was that had brought him back to haunt Delores's bedroom. But even before the ghostly boy reached the bottom step, Bernie bolted from the sofa, Mixed Blessing at his heels, rushed back into the Magruders' apartment behind the registration desk, charged down the hall, barreled through the bedroom door, and dived into bed, pulling the covers up over him.

9

Following Felicity

When Bernie woke the next morning, he was so ashamed of himself that he could hardly get out of bed. His big chance, and he'd blown it. What was he afraid of, anyway?

In spite of his mother's fears, Bernie did not really believe that the eleven-year-old ghost had come to take him away. If that were true, the ghost would have grabbed him by now. That ghost could go wherever he wanted in the whole hotel, and no one could stop him.

So what was bothering Bernie? Why hadn't he just waited till the ghost-boy got to the bottom of the stairs, then walked over and said, "Hi"? Bernie stopped tossing around in his bed and lay still. He didn't know how to talk to a ghost, that was it. There certainly weren't any books on it in the library.

"That's the problem," he said to Georgene and Weasel later, as they walked through the bus depot looking for loose change that people sometimes dropped on the floor. Weasel found a dime and Georgene found a penny, but Bernie didn't find anything.

"*What's* the problem?" asked Weasel.

"What to say to a ghost."

"I think I'd let him do the talking first," said Georgene.

Weasel started to grin. "Yeah. If he comes up to you and says 'Boo!' say, 'Boo who?' Get it? Boo hoo."

"Very funny," said Bernie. "If you aren't going to take this seriously . . ."

"Hey, Bernie, we are," Weasel said. "We just don't know any more than you do. Why don't you ask that spooky lady who lives in your hotel?"

"Felicity Jones?"

"Yeah. That young woman who goes around in a shawl," Georgene told him.

"Maybe I will," said Bernie.

That evening he sat in the living room, where he could watch the door to Felicity's room. Felicity seemed to have no trouble communicating with ghosts.

Every night after dinner, she used to take a walk up Bessledorf Hill to the parachute factory at the top, which was about as close as you could get to the sky in Indiana, and there she would sit for hours gazing at the moon.

But now, the rumors went, she walked to the cemetery instead, where her aunt and uncle were buried, and talked to their ghosts. If Bernie could follow along, maybe he would learn a little something.

Felicity came out at last and floated, almost, toward the hotel dining room. Bernie tried to walk like that, sort of gliding in on his toes.

"Got a cramp in your leg, Bernie?" one of the busboys asked.

Bernie ignored him and went on into the hotel kitchen.

"What is Felicity having for dinner?" he asked Mrs. Verona, the cook.

"Filet of flounder, a boiled potato, and asparagus," the cook told him.

Bernie went back to the apartment kitchen, where Mother was putting dinner on the table before she and Father took over their duties in the hotel dining room.

"Could I have some filet of flounder, a boiled potato, and some asparagus?" Bernie asked.

"If you want to cook it yourself," his mother said.

"If you want to eat with the rest of the family, it will be meat loaf, rice, and string beans."

Bernie ate his meat loaf. Maybe he could learn to talk with ghosts without having to be *exactly* like Felicity. He certainly hoped so.

When he went back to the hotel dining room, Felicity Jones was just getting up from the table. She floated back through the lobby again, stepped over Mixed Blessing, who was lying just inside the door, and headed for the cemetery. Bernie stayed a considerable distance behind, because Theodore had told his children that they must never spy on or otherwise annoy hotel guests.

Following Felicity wasn't exactly spying, Bernie decided. Spying was standing on a box outside somebody's window looking in. Following Felicity was just . . . uh . . . well, going in the same direction that someone else was going, twenty yards behind her, that's all.

Just inside the cemetery, Felicity Jones sat down on a large gravestone in a little circle of pine trees, and Bernie crouched down in the darkness behind her.

Felicity sat as straight as a broom, her hands on her knees, and her face tipped toward the sky. She stayed so still, so long, that Bernie wondered what would happen if he sneezed. Felicity, he imagined, would probably rise straight up into the air and come down on the other side of town.

His knees began to ache and his back and neck began to hurt from sitting so long in one position. Just when he was about ready to give up and go home, however, Felicity stopped looking at the sky and turned to her left instead.

"Well," she said aloud, to no one Bernie could see, "have you decided?"

Bernie stared.

"Uncle Herman," she continued, "you're being unfair. Aunt Imogene never said she didn't like you; she only said she couldn't stand to be in the same room with you for more than ten minutes."

Felicity suddenly turned her head in the other direction. "What, Aunt Imogene? You couldn't stay in a room with him for more than *five* minutes? Well, five minutes of liking someone is better than nothing at all."

Obviously, Bernie thought, Felicity Jones was hearing voices that he could not hear. She was still trying to settle the argument between her long-dead aunt and uncle. But what Bernie wanted to know was what to say to a ghost-boy who came down the stairs in a blue light, making the room so cold that your bones hurt.

"I tell you what," Felicity went on, "if you'll agree

to being dug up, Uncle Herman, and reburied beside Aunt Imogene, we'll lay you head to toe so that if she starts an argument, you won't have to listen."

Bernie decided that *he* didn't want to listen, either, so he got up silently and started toward the place where the Bessledorfs were buried. Maybe if *he* sat on one of their gravestones as quietly as he could, one of *their* ghosts would say something to him—something that only he could hear. And if any Bessledorf said anything at all, perhaps Bernie could find out why Jonathan kept coming back to haunt the hotel.

It was the first time Bernie had ever been in a cemetery at night by himself. Every time he stumbled over a grave marker, he found himself saying, "Excuse me." Every time he bumped into a tombstone, he said, "Oh, I'm sorry." This was stupid! This was nuts! If there were any Bessledorf ghosts around, they'd dive back underground the minute they heard him coming.

At last Bernie found the Bessledorf graves, and sat down on the tombstone of Elizabeth Myrtle, Jonathan's sister. The stone felt cold beneath him, and Bernie's teeth began to chatter.

He sat as still as he could, hands on his knees, face toward the sky, just as Felicity had sat. He waited without moving, scarcely breathing.

When at least five or six minutes had passed and he heard nothing at all, Bernie whispered, "Elizabeth?"

And after a while, "Elizabeth Bessledorf? Are you here?"

There was a rush of wind in the trees behind him, as though someone were coming, but then it passed and the night became still once more.

"Elizabeth, I'm Bernie Magruder, and I want to talk with you about Jonathan," Bernie tried again.

Did he hear a noise, or was it only the wind? Did he hear footsteps or was it just the rustle of a squirrel in the brush?

And then something touched Bernie on the arm, and he let out a yell. He grabbed at the place on his arm where he'd felt the touch, but it was only the branch of a lilac bush bobbing against him.

Disgusted with himself, Bernie got up and went home.

There was a large crowd again for the ghost tour that evening, but Bernie could tell that the whole business was beginning to wear on his family. Mother was still sleeping with Delores, Father was still sleeping with Joseph, and everyone was tense and cranky. Even the pets seemed on edge. Mixed Blessing had lumbered into the lobby the night before and accidentally stepped on Lewis. Lewis yeowed and bit Clark, and Clark took off after Salt Water, who fluttered and flew squawking about the room. What good would it do to have new banisters and new carpeting in the

parlor—to have the grandest hotel in the town of
Middleburg—if the family were too upset to enjoy it?

Somehow he had to get up his nerve to face the
ghost. Somehow he had to get up the courage to say,
"Hey, Jonathan, knock it off, will you?" But how?

10

Grave Hunting

Bernie spent the next day trying to figure out where Jonathan was buried. If there was any little patch of earth left around the hotel that wasn't covered by cement—any place at all where Jonathan could have been buried—Bernie was sure that Jonathan's mother would have left a marker of some kind—a rock on the ground, an engraving on a tree, a ribbon tied to a rosebush or something. Maybe he and Georgene and Weasel just hadn't looked hard enough.

Of course, it had all happened long ago. The stone could have been moved, the tree cut down, the ribbon rotted away in the rain. But he was going to look, anyway. Maybe finding Jonathan's grave would somehow give him courage. It would be something to talk about to Jonathan, anyway.

There were two little squares of dirt on either side of the front door to the hotel in which yew bushes grew. Bernie got down on his hands and knees and searched every inch of ground beneath one yew. He felt for stones or bricks. A small metal cross, perhaps. But he found only leaves and pebbles.

Something moved in the bushes. Bernie looked up. There was Clark, one of the Magruders' cats, staring down at him with yellow eyes.

Bernie crawled back out beneath the one yew bush and tried the other. Nothing beneath that one either, but this time Mixed Blessing came trotting around the hotel and lifted one leg above the bush.

"No!" Bernie yelled, and got out just in time.

He took the narrow sidewalk between the hotel and the funeral parlor and walked through to the little flower garden that Mrs. Verona grew behind the Bessledorf.

It was hard crawling around among the petunias and pansies, trying to feel every inch of ground for rocks or crosses or little wooden markers that might have told where a boy was buried. The roses growing along the back wall grabbed at him, catching his pants.

Something landed on Bernie, like a fifteen-pound rose with one-inch thorns.

"Yeow!" Bernie yelped, falling flat on his face in the

pansies before he saw that it was only Lewis, the other cat, who had been sitting up on the wall, waiting for someone to pounce on.

The back door opened and out came Mrs. Verona with her broom.

"Bernie Magruder!" she shrieked. "What are you doing in my pansies?" And before Bernie could tell her, the broom came down and hit him on the back.

Bernie wanted to explain about looking for the grave of the ghost-boy, but Mrs. Verona was somewhat superstitious, and even the suggestion that her pansies might be growing over somebody's grave would be enough to upset her. So Bernie gave up and went indoors. Everything was going wrong.

"What's the matter, Bernie?" his father asked that evening at dinner.

"I wish I could figure out the mystery of the ghost," Bernie said, pushing his scalloped potatoes from one side of his plate to the other.

"Well, don't try too hard," his father said. "The longer the mystery, the better for business."

Bernie and Lester exchanged glances. For the first time, Lester looked as though he might be thinking about something more than food. He stared down at his cauliflower. "Well, I feel *sorry* for the ghost," Lester said.

"The *ghost*!" exclaimed Delores.

Lester nodded.

"Well, *I* feel sorry for *me*!" Delores said. "I haven't slept in my own room for so long I probably wouldn't recognize it if I did."

"When that ghost gets tired enough of hanging around, he'll leave," Father said. "They usually do. And by then, we'll have new carpeting and new banisters. Maybe even a new chimney."

"Theodore," said Mother sternly, "I think that Bernie and Lester are right. If there's any way we can help that poor ghost-child, we should."

"Alma, my dear, what do you suggest? If I knew what the creature wanted, I'd give it to him. But if someone, ghost or not, is going to walk in our apartment every night, frighten us out of our wits, and rob us of sleep without a single explanation whatever, I do not feel guilty in the least about making a little money off him."

"Well, I'm going to find out what Jonathan wants if it takes me all summer," said Bernie.

"Fine, fine," said his father, "but do be on time for the ghost tour this evening."

Bernie was on time. He was a little early, in fact. While guests lined up at the registration desk to buy their tickets, Bernie sort of mosied down the line.

"Excuse me, ma'am," he said politely to a woman in a red dress. "But if you were to bury someone at home, where would you put him?"

The woman turned slowly and stared down at Bernie. *"What?"*

"Well, if you had a little boy and you loved him a lot . . ."

"Of *course* I'd love him!" said the woman.

"And he died . . ."

"What a thought!" said the woman's husband.

"And you buried him at home . . ." Bernie went on.

"Why on earth would we do that?" said the husband. "We'd bury him proper, in the cemetery."

"Oh," said Bernie. He caught his mother frowning at him over by the front desk, so he went outside. There he waited until he saw a group of women coming up the sidewalk toward the hotel, and before they reached the door, he went over.

"Excuse me," he said, "but if you had a little boy . . ."

"We aren't married," the largest of the women told him.

"But if you were, and you had a little boy . . ."

"I'd have girls," said the short lady in the middle. "Girls are much easier to raise."

"But if you *were* married, and you *did* have a little boy and you loved him very much and he died . . ."

"Of what?" asked the woman on the end.

"Of anything," said Bernie. "It doesn't really matter. If you were married and you had a little boy and you *did* love him very much and he died of anything at all and it would break your heart to pieces to bury him in the cemetery and you wanted to bury him at home instead, where would you put him?"

"I wouldn't touch him at all," said the first woman. "Child of mine or not, I wouldn't lay a hand on a dead person."

"Where would you *have* him buried at home, then?" Bernie persisted.

"Wouldn't have him *near* the place," said the short little woman in the middle. "Live folks belong with the living and dead folks belong with their own."

Bernie was getting nowhere. He was just about to turn away when the gray-haired woman on the end plucked his sleeve.

"If it was me, and I were to bury a child at home, I'd have him cremated. I'd put his ashes in my grandmother's cookie jar or a vase or something, and set it on the mantel. That's what I'd do."

That was a thought that had never occurred to Bernie. Maybe, somehow, Jonathan's mother had had the body cremated. If that were so, his ashes could be anywhere.

"Thank you," he told the woman. "Thank you very much."

The next day he told Georgene and Weasel what the woman had said. Weasel had never even heard of cremation, and Bernie had to explain it to him—how the corpse was burned and the ashes saved, and how it didn't hurt at all because the body had, of course, expired.

Weasel wasn't too sure about that, but he said he'd help look for Jonathan's ashes, anyway.

They started first in the attic, while the air was still somewhat cool and the attic wasn't unbearably hot.

"The ashes would be in a box or a tin or a jar about this big," Bernie explained, showing them with his hands. But although they searched every corner, behind every old chair, through the drawers of an old chest, in lamps and washbowls and broken beds and old mattresses, they couldn't find anything that looked like ashes.

They went through the third floor next. Not in the guests' rooms, of course, but they checked every drawer in every chest in the hallway, every vase in every window. They did the same on the second floor, and in the corridor of the first floor. When they came to the lobby, they made Salt Water, the parrot, move off the mantel so that they could check all the vases there. Nothing. Nothing at all.

That evening, as Mrs. Verona was getting dinner in the hotel kitchen, Bernie asked if there was anything he could do to help. The cook set him to work putting silverware on the tables, but every chance he got, Bernie opened the lids of cookie jars in the kitchen, of tea containers and coffee tins, too, looking for ashes.

"Bernie, what's got into you these days?" Mrs. Verona asked. "Seems like you're everywhere you oughtn't to be, into everything you shouldn't."

"I was just wondering," Bernie told her, "where you would keep the ashes of your dead little boy if you'd had him cremated."

Mrs. Verona made the sign of the cross on her body, picked up the salt shaker, and threw some over her shoulder. "Don't you even *mention* the dead in my kitchen, Bernie Magruder," she said. "Don't you mention them at all."

11

Face-to-Face

Bernie got up nerve enough at last to tell Georgene and Weasel about the night he had sat up to talk to Jonathan, then lost his courage.

"You actually *saw* him?" Weasel asked, and this time, when his glasses slid down his nose, he didn't even bother to push them up.

Bernie nodded.

"Could you see right through him, the way they say?" asked Georgene.

Bernie nodded again.

"What did he *look* like?"

Bernie tried to put it into words. "Like a . . . a boy made out of blue glass, I guess. Or maybe just glass, with a blue light around him. He was heading straight down the stairs toward the wall behind the registration desk."

"And Delores's bedroom is on the other side?"

"What *used* to be Delores's bedroom," Bernie sighed.

"Boy, I wish I'd see the ghost," said Georgene. They were sitting on the steps of the funeral home, sucking jawbreakers, watching the 4:00 P.M. Greyhound pull into the bus depot beyond the hotel.

"Yeah. I'll bet *I* wouldn't have run off," said Weasel.

"Good," said Bernie. "Because I want you both to stay here all night, and we'll all wait for the ghost together."

Weasel suddenly stopped sucking his jawbreaker. "When?"

"Tonight. Just bring your sleeping bag and you can sleep on the floor in my bedroom," Bernie told him. "Georgene, you can sleep on the floor in Mom's room."

"Have you *asked*?" Georgene wanted to know.

"It'll be okay," Bernie told her.

At supper, he asked.

"It's okay if Georgene and Weasel stay all night, isn't it?" he said as he passed the cooked carrots to Joseph. "They're bringing sleeping bags."

"Where's Georgene going to sleep?" Mother asked.

"Well, I thought maybe she could sleep on the floor in your bedroom, with you and Delores."

"It's a zoo already," said Delores. "One more can't hurt."

The Magruders, of course, thought it was just another sleepover. Bernie and Weasel and Georgene watched television with old Mr. Lamkin in the lobby for a while. When people arrived for the ghost tour, they helped take them around, and when the tour was over, Bernie set up the Monopoly set on the card table in one corner of the lobby, and he and Georgene and Weasel sat down to play.

But Bernie's thoughts were not on the game. Even after he got two houses on Park Place and an electric company, his eyes kept returning to the clock above the mantel, where the cats were sleeping, Lewis at one end, Clark at the other. Weasel and Georgene didn't seem to be concentrating either. Georgene passed "Go" and forgot to collect her two hundred dollars; Weasel went to jail and didn't even seem to care.

One by one the hotel guests put down their newspapers or magazines, set down their cups of coffee, said good-night to each other and to Bernie's mother, who was sitting at the registration desk rewriting the last chapter of *Quivering Lips*. One by one they went off to bed, until only Bernie and his friends, Mother, Felicity Jones, and Mrs. Buzzwell were left in the lobby.

"I have some wonderful news," Felicity said to

Mother, stopping by the desk on the way to her room. "I have just come from the cemetery, and my dear departed Uncle Herman and Aunt Imogene have reached a reconciliation."

Mother looked up warily.

"Uncle Herman has agreed to be dug up and reburied alongside Aunt Imogene, as long as he can be six inches higher. For the first time that anyone can remember, they have both actually agreed about something."

"How nice," said Mother. "What a wonderful feeling that must be." She watched open-mouthed as Felicity half-floated down the hall to her room.

When Joseph came into the lobby to lock up, Mother said, "Joseph, that Felicity is a strange one, I tell you. Do you think it's possible that *she* has something to do with our ghost-boy, that *she* could have brought him here?"

"Felicity has lived at the hotel longer than we have, Mother," Bernie heard his older brother say. "I don't see why she would start something like that now."

"Well, don't you go falling in love with her," Mrs. Magruder warned. "I can tell by the way she looks at you sometimes that she likes you."

Joseph only laughed. "You've got your mind on love, Mom. You must be finishing your romance novel."

"I know the signs," Mother said. "Remember that

night she had us sitting around the kitchen table, trying to contact the ghost? I saw the way she sat down by you. I saw the way she put her fingers against yours."

"Well, maybe so, Mom, but right now my mind's on finishing college and becoming a veterinarian, not on some babe who's out to lunch."

"Out to *lunch?*" Georgene whispered to Bernie.

"A little bit loony," Bernie explained.

"I'll tell you one thing," said Mrs. Buzzwell, lifting her large bottom off her chair. "This is the strangest place I have ever lived. First we thought there was a mad gasser on the loose in Middleburg, and that he was living right here at the Bessledorf. Next those bodies kept appearing in bedrooms, and now we have a ghost. If there are many more strange happenings, Mrs. Magruder, I shall find another place to live."

Why don't you? thought Bernie.

But Mother just clucked and patted Mrs. Buzzwell's arm as she passed the desk. "Mrs. Buzzwell, my dear, you know we wouldn't let anything happen to you. You are perfectly safe with my Theodore in charge," she said.

"Humph," said Mrs. Buzzwell, and went on back to her room.

Bernie wondered how Mother could promise that. *No* one knew what would happen next, not even Father.

"Well, any time you're ready for bed, Georgene,"

Mother said, "you just bring your sleeping bag into my bedroom. Delores and I will be in bed, but you sleep wherever you like on the floor."

"I will, Mrs. Magruder, but we want to finish this game first," Georgene said politely.

As soon as Bernie and his friends were alone, Weasel said, "How soon will the ghost come, Bernie?"

"Sometimes he doesn't come at all," Bernie said. "But if we're lucky, it's somewhere between midnight and two."

"And we're supposed to drag you bodily over to the stairs when he appears?"

"Yes," said Bernie.

Weasel and Georgene looked at him.

"I mean it," said Bernie. "When the blue light starts down the stairs, you get on one side of me, Weasel, and you get on the other, Georgene, and see that I get over to those stairs and stay there till we find out what Jonathan wants."

They tried to finish the Monopoly game, but it wasn't any use. Just before midnight, they put the game away.

Salt Water, the parrot, slept on beneath the cover on his cage. Lewis and Clark, on opposite ends of the mantel, slept, too. Mixed Blessing, lying on the door-mat, his paws jerking every so often, his jowls twitching, dreamed of rabbits and squirrels. The clock struck twelve. Bernie and Georgene and Weasel went over to the couch, sat down, and waited.

They whispered back and forth to each other until twelve-thirty, their eyes on the stairs. But when one o'clock came, Bernie began to feel a little silly. What if this was one of the nights that the ghost-boy didn't come? In fact, maybe he wouldn't come just because Georgene and Weasel were there. Weasel's head was already tipping a little to one side—his eyelids drooping lower and lower.

And then, when Bernie was just about to give up and tell them both to go to bed and forget about it, Bernie felt a draft. Georgene grabbed hold of Bernie's arm on one side, Weasel grabbed his knee on the other, and the three of them sat there shaking.

"Is it J-Jonathan?" Weasel asked.

"I think so," said Bernie. Three pairs of eyes studied the stairs. On the mantel, Lewis and Clark sat up, looking around. Under the cloth cover, Salt Water began to fidget in his cage. Mixed Blessing opened one eye, got up from the mat by the door, and came over to Bernie. He lay down by Bernie's feet and whined.

"H-he's coming, all right!" Bernie whispered.

"Let's go, then," said Georgene, tugging at Bernie.

Weasel stood up too, but his legs gave out from under him and he sat down again.

"Come *on!*" Georgene said, pulling him up. And

then to Bernie: "It's your chance! You've g-got to talk to him!"

A blue light appeared at the top of the stairs. The room grew colder still. Bernie, Georgene, and Weasel froze in their tracks. As the blue light came down the stairs, Bernie whispered. *"Go, feet, go!"*

His feet wouldn't move.

"Pull me!" he said to Weasel.

"I'm t-trying!" Weasel said, his teeth chattering.

Georgene gave a tug, Weasel gave a tug, and finally Bernie found himself walking across the lobby.

Step by step they approached the stairs, where the ghost was descending. They kept going until they stood in a row at the very foot of the stairs, blocking Jonathan's path.

Bernie looked up. The ghost-boy came closer and closer. Bernie could see him clearly now. He was Bernie's age, all right, but he didn't look very much like Bernie. He was a little thinner for one thing, a little taller, and though Bernie could see right through him like glass, his hair was a little lighter than Bernie's, his eyes a little darker.

All the things Bernie had thought of to say to Jonathan seemed to have slipped from his head. He stared at the eyes of the ghost-boy, and the ghost-boy stared back.

On the ghost came, as though Bernie weren't even

there. He was on the third step from the bottom, then the second step from the bottom. Bernie tried to move his mouth but nothing happened. His tongue wouldn't budge, and even when he opened his lips, nothing came out.

He felt a great coldness as the blue light reached the first step from the bottom and he was face to face with Jonathan. A great sweep of coldness passed through Bernie's body. He felt Georgene letting go of his arm on one side, Weasel letting go on the other. For a moment or two, Bernie thought he had frozen to death, that he was a statue made of ice. Then he felt warmth coming back into his feet and hands.

Slowly he turned around. Georgene was still there. So was Weasel. Mixed Blessing was licking one of his hands, and the cats' green eyes gleamed at him from the mantel. The ghost-boy had walked right through him but, once again, he was gone.

12

"Jonathan, Meet Bernie"

Bernie and his friends didn't eat much at breakfast. Bernie stared down at his pancake, making little holes in it with his fork, Georgene dug a little well in the center of hers and filled it full of syrup, and Weasel pushed his back and forth across his plate.

"The three of you look half-dead," Mother commented as she poured some milk in their glasses. "That must have been some Monopoly game last night. I didn't even hear you come in my room, Georgene."

Bernie, Georgene, and Weasel exchanged glances. "Mom," said Bernie, "the ghost came again last night. We saw him."

The rest of the family looked up.

"Wow!" said Lester, admiringly. "What'd he look like, Bernie?"

"He's about as old as me, just like Delores said. But his hair's lighter and his eyes are darker, and you can see right through him like glass. I think he's trying to tell us something."

"Well, I'd certainly like to tell *him* a thing or two," said Delores. "Namely, to get the heck out of my bedroom."

"I tried to talk to him," Bernie said.

"Oh, *Bernie!*" said his mother, sitting down with a plop. "You *know* how worried I am about you!"

"Bernie, my boy, what happened?" asked Theodore.

"Last week, one night when I couldn't sleep, I was sitting on the couch in the lobby when the room got very cold and I saw him come down the stairs in a blue light. But I couldn't get up my nerve to go talk to him, so I asked Georgene and Weasel to stay up with me last night. Jonathan came again, so we all went over to the bottom of the stairs, and when he reached the bottom step . . ." Bernie took a deep breath.

"What *happened?*" cried Mother and Father and Delores and Joseph and Lester all together.

"He went right through me. It was like I'd swallowed a cup of snow. My whole body got cold, but he passed right out the other side of me and disappeared through the wall into Delores's room."

"Bernie, he could have snatched you away forever!" Mother wept.

"You should have *told* us before you tried something like that!" said Father sternly.

"I guess I should have," Bernie admitted. "But I'm telling you now. If Jonathan was going to spirit me away, that was a perfect opportunity. But he didn't. I *know* he's here for a reason, Dad, and I want to find out what. I think he wants us to go into Delores's bedroom with him, and maybe he'll talk to us there."

"Oh, Bernie," Mother cried, and her tears were flowing now. "If anything should happen to you . . . ! I would never be happy again, not even if *Quivering Lips* became a best-seller."

"Alma," said Theodore, "I think that Bernie is right. If the ghost had any intention of taking him, Bernie wouldn't be sitting at the table with us now. If he wants to try to talk to the ghost-boy in Delores's bedroom tonight, I think we should let him."

"I want Georgene and Weasel with me," said Bernie. He could hear Weasel gulp.

"I myself shall be right outside the door," Theodore promised, "and if you need me, Bernie, all you need do is yell."

"You'll fall asleep, Theodore," said Mother.

"I'll sit up with him," Joseph promised.

"I want to stay up, too," said Lester.

"Well, I won't be able to sleep if everyone else is up," Delores complained. "I don't know how I'll ever manage to be Worker of the Week if this keeps on."

"We shall *all* sit up," said Mother. "If Georgene and Weasel can sleep over again, we'll let Bernie wait in Delores's room tonight and see what the ghost-boy wants."

At that moment Mixed Blessing began to bark. There was a commotion out front, and then the sound of someone rapping on the registration desk with a cane.

Theodore leaped from his chair and opened the door of the apartment. There in the lobby stood Mr. Fairchild, the owner, and he was looking very, very pleased.

"Come in, come in," said Theodore, as the man in the gray suit strode into the kitchen. "You know my family, of course, and these are friends of my son Bernie—Georgene and Weasel."

"Very glad to know you," said Mr. Fairchild, shaking their hands hard. "Very glad indeed. Magruder, I simply had to come down from Indianapolis and tell you how happy I am with the job you are doing as manager of my hotel. A fine job! A splendid job! Ever since the story of the ghost appeared in the paper, the hotel has been doing more business than ever. I hope the tours last a long, long time."

Bernie and Georgene and Weasel looked at each other.

"I'm afraid that's not possible."

There was another voice in the room. Bernie turned around. There in the apartment doorway stood Felicity Jones.

"What?" asked Mr. Fairchild. And then, turning to Father, "Who is this young woman?"

"Felicity Jones, one of the regulars," said Theodore.

"Excuse me, Mr. Magruder," Felicity said, "but I couldn't help hearing what this man said, and I think you all ought to know that there is a very good chance that this ghost you have been seeing will simply fade away."

"Then we must keep him coming at all costs," said Mr. Fairchild.

Felicity shook her head. "Some fade, some don't," she said. "When a ghost wants something badly, and he gets it, he often goes away. But even if he doesn't get what he wants, he sometimes loses heart, just as *we* lose heart, and gives up. You can tell when it's happening because his light starts to fade."

"Well, then, you must be sure that whatever the ghost comes for, he doesn't get," Mr. Fairchild boomed. "If he loses heart, there's nothing much we

can do about that, but if you know what this ghost-
boy is after, Magruder, for goodness' sake don't give
it to him. Keep him coming!"

Mother got slowly to her feet. "Mr. Fairchild, sir,
with all respect, I find that a terrible idea," she said.
"This poor boy has come to tell us something, and it
is up to us to find out what. We made a success of
your hotel long before the ghost appeared, and we
shall go on making a success of your hotel long after
he's gone. But if there is any way we can relieve Jonathan Bessledorf's suffering, if that's who the ghost-
boy is, we shall do so."

"Well said, Alma," Theodore added. "I must admit
that I got carried away when I saw how much money
those tours were bringing in. But that's a poor excuse
for making a child suffer."

Mr. Fairchild sat down hard in one of the kitchen
chairs. "He's not a child, he's a ghost! He's had his
chance as a child. If he wants to come back and haunt
this hotel, that's his problem."

Bernie couldn't help himself. "He didn't get a very
big chance, Mr. Fairchild. He only got eleven years."

Mr. Fairchild turned and looked at Bernie.

Lester stopped licking the grape jelly off his toast
and chimed in. "Yeah. If you had broken *your* neck
when *you* were eleven, Mr. Fairchild, where would
you be now?"

"Boys . . . !" said Theodore sternly.

But Mr. Fairchild stopped him. "Magruder, they are absolutely right. If I had broken my neck when I was eleven, I would not be the owner of this hotel, that's certain. People will lose interest in the ghost eventually, anyway, and stop coming, so the tours are only a temporary attraction. If you can figure out what the ghost-boy wants, then give it to him. Yes, sir. By all means, give it to him. And you shall have your new carpeting and your new banisters and even a new chimney, if that's what you want."

With that, Mr. Fairchild stood up, picked up his cane, and went striding back outside to where his cab was waiting.

"Whew!" said Joseph. "That was close."

"Now all we have to do is help Jonathan," said Bernie.

"So we can all go back to our own bedrooms and get some sleep," said Father.

"So I can become Worker of the Week," said Delores.

Georgene and Weasel went to the telephone to call home and ask if they could sleep over once again.

Nobody felt like playing Monopoly that evening. Waiting out in the lobby on the couch for the ghost to pass by was one thing. But the thought of waiting for the ghost in Delores's room was another.

There was something about the ghost tour that evening that brought goose bumps out on Bernie's arms. When he led the group of guests into Delores's bedroom and looked at the candle burning on the little stand at the foot of her bed, he realized that in a few hours, that's exactly where he and Georgene and Weasel would be sitting. And at midnight, that's exactly where they were.

"I'm scared, Bernie," Georgene admitted.

"So am I," said Weasel. "Before I was just medium petrified. Now I'm petrified out of my mind."

Bernie tried to keep his own voice from shaking. "Just remember that if he had really wanted to hurt any of us, he could have last night by the stairs. I think he was trying to get us to follow him."

"So he could hurt us in here?" asked Weasel.

"So he could tell us what it is he wants," said Bernie.

"All right, Jonathan," said Georgene, as she stretched out her legs on the floor. "Do your stuff. We're waiting."

Outside the bedroom door, Bernie knew, his family had gathered. He could hear the steady *thump, thump,* of Mixed Blessing's tail on the floorboards. He and Georgene and Weasel sat in a row at the foot of Delores's bed, between the bed frame and the little table with the candle on it.

Bernie looked at his watch. Twelve-fifteen. The *thump* in the hallway stopped finally, and he knew that

Mixed Blessing had gone to sleep. Twelve-thirty. Footsteps going down the hall to his bedroom told him that Lester had given up and was going to bed. Twelve forty-five. The soft clink and clank from the kitchen told him that Mother was making a new pot of coffee.

And then, about one o'clock, he felt a draft on his legs and arms. Georgene and Weasel turned and looked at him. The room got colder and colder. Outside in the hallway, Mixed Blessing began to whine.

And then, a faint blue light appeared on the wall opposite. Bernie and Georgene and Weasel stared as it grew brighter and brighter, and finally the ghost-boy came through the wall and began walking slowly toward them.

Bernie had to clench his jaw tightly to keep his teeth from chattering. Both Georgene and Weasel had grabbed onto one of his knees and were clutching them as though afraid they might all blow away.

On came the ghost-boy, his eyes right on Bernie— left foot, right foot, left foot, right . . .

When he got to the little table with the candle on it, he stopped and stared down at the three children there on the floor.

Bernie heard Georgene gulp.

"Jonathan," she said, "meet Bernie. Bernie, this is Jonathan."

13

Twenty Questions

The ghost-boy came no further.

He looked even more like glass than he had before. But his eyes looked just as intently at Bernie, then at Georgene and Weasel, and back to Bernie again. Bernie felt Georgene nudge him with her elbow.

"Are you J-Jonathan Bessledorf?" Bernie managed to say. "Was this your house?"

The ghost-boy did not answer.

"We want to help you," Bernie said. "We think you've come here to tell us something, but we don't know what."

Still the ghost stood silently, as though listening to every word.

Bernie tried again. "You're Jonathan Bessledorf, aren't you? You died from a fall down the stairs, and you want to tell us something. This is my friend Weasel, and this is my friend Georgene, and if there is anything we can do to help you, we will. But we have to know what it is you want."

For another minute, two minutes, almost, the ghost-boy stood like a blue ice statue. And then finally he lifted his arms up over his head.

"Look!" Georgene whispered. "What does he mean?"

"I don't know," said Bernie. "That's what he did when Joseph was in here. Just put his arms in the air."

They stared at the ghost-boy.

"Can you speak?" Bernie asked finally, feeling a little more courageous.

The ghost-boy looked down at him and slowly, slowly, shook his head.

Bernie's heart began to pound. At least they were communicating.

"I-I don't know very much about ghosts," Bernie said, "so you'll have to help us. *Are* you Jonathan Bessledorf?"

Slowly, slowly, the ghost nodded.

"And you want something upstairs?"

The ghost-boy looked very disappointed, and put his arms back down.

"Oh, please don't stop!" Georgene begged. "We really want to help you. Try again."

This time Jonathan looked at her with his blue-glass eyes, and then he raised his arms a second time. The room was growing colder all the time.

"You want something very big," Georgene guessed, tugging the spread off the bed and pulling it around her shoulders.

The ghost-boy gave no reply.

"He must mean no," said Weasel.

"It's not upstairs, then, and it's not big?" Bernie asked.

"Is it animal, vegetable, or mineral?" asked Weasel.

Bernie gave him a poke. How was the ghost supposed to answer if he couldn't speak?

"Okay, is it animal?" Weasel asked.

The ghost boy just looked at him.

"Is it vegetable?" Weasel asked.

No answer.

"Mineral?"

"Weasel, he doesn't even know what you're talking about. He probably never even played that game," said Georgene. "Look, Jonathan," she added, turning to the ghost. "This thing you want. Is it smaller than a pillow?"

The ghost didn't move.

"Larger than a loaf of bread?" asked Bernie.

Jonathan put down his arms again, and Bernie didn't know whether or not he imagined it, but the ghost looked very sad.

"Please keep trying," Bernie begged. "We'll stay here all night if we need to."

But even as he spoke, he saw that Jonathan was growing dimmer and dimmer, and finally, in the place where the ghost had stood, there was nothing but a pale blue light, and then even that was gone.

Bernie felt like crying. "I didn't want him to go!" he said. "I just couldn't understand what it was he wanted."

"What could he have meant?" Georgene wondered, and she sounded as though she were about to cry, too.

"You know what?" said Weasel. "I'm not the least bit scared of him anymore. I just wish we could help him."

They got up off the floor, which felt like the floor of a refrigerator, and opened the door.

Bernie's family was standing anxiously outside.

"Oh, my sweet, you're all right," said his mother, grabbing him and kissing him in front of Georgene and Weasel. Georgene was polite and pretended she didn't notice, but Weasel grinned.

"What happened?" asked Theodore.

"We didn't find out anything," Bernie said disappointedly. "Except that he really is Jonathan Bessledorf and this was his house. We asked him questions about what he wanted, but all he did was raise his arms, just like he did for Joseph."

"He's going to drive us mad, Mother!" Delores said. "Stark raving mad! *That's* what he's come for."

"Delores, hush," said her father. "He could have done a lot worse. When he raises his arms, he must mean something. We just haven't guessed it yet."

"I'm afraid he'll give up," said Bernie, and then he remembered what Felicity had said about a ghost losing heart and slowly fading away. "If that happens, we'll never know, and Jonathan will never find what he came for."

"*I'm* afraid we'll lose sleep!" said Delores. "And if I don't sleep, I can't work, and if I can't work, I'll never make Worker of the Week, and if I don't make Worker of the Week, *I* will fade away."

"Don't be selfish," said her mother.

But Delores would not be hushed up. "How do we know there aren't more of them, Mother? How do we know that the whole Bessledorf tribe isn't going to show up here one by one, just like the animals Joseph brings home from the veterinarian college?"

"I think they would have come by now," Joseph told her. "Perhaps we should have a talk with Felicity Jones. She knows about spirits. She may be able to help."

"Not *you*, Joseph!" warned his mother. "That girl has eyes for you. The next thing you know, you'll be married to her, and we'll have a lot of ghostly grandchildren wandering about this hotel."

"Well, let Bernie talk to her, then," said Joseph. "Somebody ought to, before Jonathan loses heart."

"That's true," said Mrs. Magruder. "Let's all go to bed now, and tomorrow, Bernie, I want you to have a long, polite talk with Felicity Jones."

Bernie waited two hours the next morning for Felicity, and when she finally came out of her room, he followed her into the dining room and asked if she would mind if he sat at her table.

"Not at all, Bernie," she said. "I am feeling very shaky this morning and would welcome the company. The whole night seemed unsettled, and it's as though I hardly slept at all."

"We didn't sleep much, either," Bernie told her. And then he explained how he and his friends had waited for Jonathan in Delores's room, and how they hadn't learned much at all.

"Poor, poor child," Felicity said of Jonathan as she ate her Cream of Wheat.

"I'm afraid he'll lose heart, Felicity!" Bernie told her. "I *know* he's come here to tell us something, but we just can't seem to guess. We asked if it was animal, vegetable, or mineral, and he didn't even know what we were talking about. Then we asked if it was smaller than a pillow or larger than a loaf of bread. That didn't get us anywhere, either."

"Perhaps it's not an 'it,' " said Felicity.

"What?" said Bernie.

"Perhaps what Jonathan has come for is not something that you can see, exactly, or even hold in the palm of your hand. Perhaps he came to ask a favor. They do that, sometimes."

"How can we do him a favor when we don't even know what he wants?"

Felicity thought about it for a while as she took another spoonful of Cream of Wheat. She ate her toast without butter, her Cream of Wheat without sugar, and drank her coffee without any cream. Bernie couldn't help but think there would be a lot more zip to Felicity Jones if she added a little more zap to her food. But he was trying to be very polite, as his mother had said.

"Sometimes, until a ghost can really trust you," she said at last, "they tell you only a little bit at a time. Perhaps if you are very patient, Jonathan will show you a little bit more the next time he comes."

"I hope so," said Bernie. And he went to the phone to call Georgene and Weasel again, and arrange the third overnight of the summer.

14

Not a Minute to Lose

So once again Bernie and Georgene and Weasel waited. And once again the Magruder family gathered outside Delores's bedroom door, in case Bernie should need them.

Mother had suggested that perhaps they should take Felicity in with them, but Felicity said it was clear to her that Jonathan Bessledorf felt comfortable with Bernie and his friends. He might not be so comfortable with her there. Bernie could understand that, all right.

Twelve became one, and one became two, and Bernie worried that perhaps this time, Jonathan would not come. It was almost two-thirty when a chill swept over the room. The Magruders out in the hall felt it, too, for Bernie heard Delores say, "It's freezing in here, Mother! How can it *get* so cold in the middle of July?"

"Shhh," came Mother's voice.

But this time, when the pale blue light came through the wall opposite Bernie and Georgene and Weasel, Bernie's heart leaped up in his chest, for it did not seem to get any brighter once it was in the room. The ghost-boy appeared as usual, but he was much fainter than he had been before; Bernie could see his face all right, but it was a little bit blurred, like ice that was beginning to melt. Jonathan, the ghost-boy, was losing heart.

"Please don't give up," he told the ghost. "We really do want to help you. We're trying as hard as we can."

The ghost-boy stood in his usual place at the foot of the bed. Once again he lifted his arms, but this time his wrists were bent, the palms of his hands facing upward, as though he were holding something large and heavy.

"What do you have in your hands, Jonathan?" Bernie asked. "Is it big?"

Jonathan nodded.

"Is it heavy?" asked Weasel.

Jonathan nodded again, and Bernie could have sworn he saw tears in the ghost-boy's eyes. Were they tears, or was he melting? Bernie didn't know, but he was very much afraid that soon there would be nothing left of the ghost-boy at all.

"Is it a tray?" asked Georgene.

The ghost-boy shook his head.

"Is it bigger than a chair?" asked Weasel.

Jonathan nodded.

"Bigger than a bed?" asked Bernie.

Jonathan nodded again, and he seemed to be very excited.

"How could he be holding something bigger than a bed?" Georgene asked Bernie. "He couldn't even be holding that."

But Bernie felt they were on the right track. "Bigger than a *house?*" he asked.

The ghost-boy dropped his arms suddenly. Slowly he shook his head, and then he began to fade.

"Wait!" Bernie cried. "Please come back, Jonathan. We'll stay here as long as you need." But the pale blue light grew even fainter, and finally the ghost-boy was gone.

"I feel like bawling," said Georgene.

"Maybe that's the end of him," said Weasel.

"It *can't* be the end of him," said Bernie. "It just *can't.*"

But when they went out in the hallway where the family waited, Mrs. Magruder seemed to think it was over, too. "You know what Felicity said, Bernie," she told him. "When a ghost loses heart, he begins to fade. And there's just nothing we can do."

"But he came all the way back here to tell us something."

"Well, then, perhaps we'll never know," said Theodore. "Let's get some sleep."

The next night Georgene and Weasel stayed over and the night after that, but although they waited in Delores's room until almost four in the morning, Jonathan never came.

The next evening after dinner Bernie felt so bad that he walked to Middleburg Cemetery by himself and didn't even ask Georgene and Weasel along. It was as though he had lost a friend. Jonathan had never said a single word to him, and yet Bernie felt they would have been friends somehow if they had both lived in the same time. He was sitting on a rock inside the gate when Felicity walked in and sat down beside him.

"I hope you don't mind that I followed you here, Bernie," she said, "but you looked so very sad. I thought perhaps I might recite a poem for you. Do you mind?"

The last thing in the world Bernie wanted to hear was a poem, especially any poem that Felicity Jones had made up, which were the only ones she ever recited. But he tried his best to be polite, so he just shrugged. He couldn't bring himself to actually say yes.

Felicity closed her eyes and tipped her head back:

"Little ghost with face of blue,
How I want to talk to you.
How I want to hold your hand,
Read your words and understand."

Bernie had felt like crying before, and now he actually felt the tears well up. He wished that Felicity would stop, but she didn't:

"No more footsteps on the stairs,
No more rustles of the chairs.
You are gone without a clue,
Little ghost with face of blue."

"Shut up," said Bernie.

The words seemed to hang there in the air. He couldn't believe he had been so rude, but one more rhyme out of Felicity, and he'd be bawling, he was sure of it.

The strange part was that Felicity didn't seem to mind. In fact, Bernie was not even sure she had heard, because she seemed to be listening to someone else.

"Listen!" she said suddenly. "Uncle Herman is talking. Oh, I do hope he's not quarreling with Aunt Imogene again, after all I've done for them."

Bernie had no trouble being quiet. He just wished that Felicity would be quiet, too.

"They're talking to each other," she said at last. "They're wondering where Jonathan could have gone."

"They know Jonathan?" Bernie asked. He spoke in spite of himself.

"Well, they *are* all dead, you know," Felicity said. "But if they know Jonathan, and they see that he's gone from wherever it is that their spirits dwell, it can only mean one thing: that he's coming back here— one more time, anyway."

"What will I do, Felicity?" Bernie asked. "We just can't guess what he's trying to tell us!" And he explained how hard they had tried to guess what Jonathan was holding in his hands, but couldn't.

Felicity thought it over. "Perhaps he's not holding something at all," she said at last. "Maybe if you try to guess what Jonathan is *doing*, you will come a little closer to it."

"Thanks," Bernie said, and got up and ran home.

"This is the last night I can sleep here," Georgene said as she arrived one more time with her sleeping bag. "Mom says if I don't sleep at home soon, I won't recognize my own bed when I see it."

"You and me both," said Delores.

There was something very different about the ghost

tour that night. The Magruders felt it; the guests felt it; Salt Water and Lewis and Clark and Mixed Blessing felt it. Sort of an electricity in the air, as though someone or something else were present. Bernie didn't even have to guess: It was Jonathan.

When the ghost tour was over and the hotel guests had gone to bed, he and Georgene and Weasel took their places once again in Delores's bedroom. This time Lester vowed he would stay up if he had to stay up all night. The Magruders sat on folding chairs out in the hall, beyond the door to Delores's room. Everyone waited.

Midnight came. Then one, then two, then three. But Bernie wasn't worried. The electricity was still there. He could feel it. At three-thirty, the room grew cold—colder than it had ever been before, as though someone had opened the front door during a blizzard.

The pale blue light came through the opposite wall once again, and just as Bernie feared, it was paler than ever.

"Try hard, Jonathan," Bernie begged. "Please stay here until we guess."

The ghost-boy put his arms up once again, palms turned upward.

This time Bernie did what Felicity had suggested. He quit trying to guess what it was Jonathan had in his hands, and tried to figure out what it was that

Jonathan was doing instead. In fact, he got to his feet and put his hands up just like Jonathan. He watched the ghost-boy and did exactly what he did.

The ghost boy bent his knees and pushed upward with his hands.

"Are you pushing, Jonathan?" Bernie asked.

The ghost-boy's face seemed wildly excited. He nodded.

"He's pushing!" Weasel said.

"Pushing something up?" asked Georgene.

Jonathan seemed confused.

"Pushing something . . . open?" asked Bernie.

Jonathan nodded again.

"Is it bigger than a boat?" asked Weasel, and the ghost boy put his arms down.

"No!" yelled Bernie. "Don't give up, Jonathan. Please! Just tell us where it is, whatever it is. Is it in this house, Jonathan?"

The ghost-boy nodded once again, but before Bernie could question him further, he began to fade.

"No!" cried Bernie and Georgene and Weasel all together, but they couldn't stop him.

This time, however, instead of disappearing back into the wall, the ghost-boy sank through the floor and on into the cellar.

15

The Fading Blue Light

"Come on!" yelled Bernie. "We've got to follow him! We can't let him go like this. We've got to guess."

He charged out into the hallway, Weasel and Georgene behind him.

"Bernie . . . !" said Mother.

"We can't stop!" Bernie told her. "Jonathan needs us!"

He rushed to the kitchen and flung open the door to the cellar. The Magruders followed. All the shouting and running woke some of the other guests, and down the stairs came old Mr. Lamkin in his pajamas, Mrs. Buzzwell in her blue bathrobe, and Felicity Jones in her silk kimono.

"Turn on the lights!" Bernie said. "There must be

something here! Jonathan was trying to tell us, even when he faded away. The secret must be here in the cellar."

"But where, Bernie?" said his mother. "There's nothing much down there."

Father flicked on the lights, and indeed it seemed to be true. The cellar was very much in order—a few boxes here, a shovel there, a few screens, some paint, the furnace, the water heater . . . nothing that would vaguely interest a ghost.

Bernie looked around quickly for a trace of the pale blue light. It was gone. But the cellar was very cold, colder than it had ever been, and Bernie knew that Jonathan had been here.

"We've lost him!" Georgene said sadly.

It couldn't be! Not after all of this. Bernie looked desperately about. What was it Jonathan wanted him to know? Was that the last time he would ever see the ghost-boy? Bernie thought of all the things he had wanted to ask Jonathan Bessledorf, beginning with where he was buried.

Where he was buried.

Bernie stood absolutely still and looked about. Here? Was it possible that Jonathan's mother had buried her son in the cellar?

Of course! Until this summer, the floor in the cellar had been dirt. When the Bessledorfs were living here, Mrs. Bessledorf must have picked up the body of her youngest child and carried him down to the cellar, dug the hole, and buried him herself to keep him near her always.

"He's here!" Bernie yelled.

"Where?" asked Theodore, looking around.

"Here! Under the cement!" said Bernie. "I know it, Dad! This is where Jonathan is buried."

"Bernie, are you sure?" asked Mother.

"That's what he was trying to tell us. He was lifting something with his hands—something big and heavy. We've covered up his grave."

Mother turned to Felicity Jones. "My dear, what do you think? Is that enough to upset a ghost?"

"No one likes to be forgotten, Mrs. Magruder," Felicity said. "If you were six feet under, would you want a foot of concrete . . . ?"

"Never mind," said Theodore. "If Jonathan is under this floor, we will uncover him—his grave, that is. But how do we know where it is?"

"Every time I came down here barefoot to do the wash, I stubbed my toe," said Delores thoughtfully.

"There was something over there near the water heater," said Joseph. "I brought a baby pigeon down here one night to keep it warm near the water heater, and I remember tripping over a rock or something in the dirt floor. It could have been a sunken grave marker."

"Yes, I remember now," said Mother, walking over. "It was right about here."

"I fell and banged my knee on it once," said Lester. "I thought it was a brick."

"It *must* have been a grave marker!" Bernie told them.

"Get a jackhammer!" yelled old Mr. Lamkin excitedly from the stairs.

"Call the rescue squad," suggested Mrs. Buzzwell.

"My dear friends and family," said Theodore. "Before we get a jackhammer and dig up the whole floor, where exactly is this grave of Jonathan's? Where was the something you tripped over?"

"Here," said Lester, pointing.

"No, over there," said Delores.

"I think you're both wrong; it's about here," said Joseph.

"Bernie," said Weasel. "Feel! Here!" Bernie walked over where Weasel was squatting and put out his hand beside Weasel's. It was very, very cold over one particular part of the concrete floor. It was somewhat near the washer, but closer to the water heater, and when the others saw where Bernie and Weasel were pointing, they agreed that yes, that was about the place they had tripped or stumbled or stubbed their toes.

"It all makes sense," said Mother. "When Delores saw the ghost-boy for the first time, it was about a week after we had put the new cement floor in the cellar."

"He was all covered up," said Lester.

"Forgotten," said Bernie.

"I feel a poem coming on," said Felicity Jones. A moan went through the little crowd assembled there in the basement, but Felicity ignored it:

"Oh, ghostly child whose tender face
Will grace us nevermore;
Thy soul was held a prisoner
Right here beneath the floor."

"That will do, Felicity," said Father. "Bernie, go wake Wilbur Wilkins right now and tell him to get his jackhammer."

"Right now?" asked Bernie.

"Right this very minute. We won't make Jonathan lie under a foot of concrete any longer than he has to."

Bernie ran upstairs to the lobby and down the hall to the room at the end where the hotel handyman slept. Wilbur Wilkins could sleep through a hurricane, but at last Bernie's pounding roused him.

"You've got to come!" Bernie gasped. "And bring your jackhammer!" And he hurried back to the cellar.

Wilbur Wilkins stood at the top of the stairs, a pair of overalls pulled up over his red-striped pajamas, and wiped his eyes with one hand, holding his jackhammer in the other.

"What in tarnation is going on?" he said. "Like to wake the dead."

"Well, that's just about what we're trying to do," Theodore told him, and pointed to a chalk line he had drawn on the concrete floor. "We want this patch of concrete dug up, Wilbur, and do it gently, if you please."

Wilbur came sleepily down the stairs, muttering to himself. "First they want the cement; then they don't want the cement. Wake a man in the middle of the night, and the whole town of Middleburg, while they're at it."

"Wouldn't miss it for the world!" said Mr. Lamkin.

Wilbur Wilkins started the jackhammer, and it sounded as though the whole hotel were coming down. It wasn't long before Officer Feeney appeared at the top of the stairs, waving his arms and moving his mouth, but no one could hear what he was saying, so Wilbur Wilkins just kept at his work until the little two-by-five plot of concrete had crumbled.

The noise shut off at last.

Feeney was beside himself. He leaned over and looked down the basement steps. "You realize you're breaking the noise ordinance, Magruder?" he bellowed.

"So are you, Feeney, but we've had a little problem here, and I think we've solved it now."

"Still ghost-chasing, I'll bet," said the policeman.

"Why, a ghost could lean over your shoulder and eat off your plate and the only thing you'd notice, like as not, was a little draft about the head."

"Maybe," said Theodore. "Maybe."

Bernie got a flashlight, and he and Georgene and Weasel got down on their hands and knees and began removing chunks of concrete, until they were down to bare dirt once again.

Bernie searched around in the rubble until he found the corner of a brick or a stone or a marker sticking up out of the dirt, just the way it had always stuck out before. No one had ever bothered to get a light and see what it was.

Bernie grabbed Mixed Blessing by the collar and pulled him over. "Dig," he said. "Carefully," he added.

Mixed Blessing dug, but not so carefully, and the dirt flew. When Bernie figured the dog had dug enough, he stopped him and uncovered the rest of the marker with his hands. Then he turned the flashlight on the marker once again and read the words:

JONATHAN, MY LIFE, MY JOY

For a long time everyone was quiet. Even Feeney came softly down the stairs, stared at the marker, and removed his hat.

"Well," said Lester finally. "Jonathan's remembered now."

"We won't forget him," said Bernie.

"Now instead of stumbling over one little corner of a grave marker, we can fall right into the grave," said Delores.

"We can put a fence around it, can't we, Mr. Wilkins?" Bernie asked.

"First they want cement, then they don't want cement, then they want a fence . . ." said the handyman, going back upstairs and taking his jackhammer with him.

"Do you suppose I can have my room back?" Delores asked, yawning.

"Try it and see," said Mrs. Magruder. "I'm sure we are all so tired that we will sleep anywhere."

"I'll help you build that fence tomorrow, Bernie," Lester said, going back upstairs.

One by one everyone went up to the rooms above until only Bernie, Georgene, and Weasel were left in the cellar.

"I never would have guessed that was what he was holding in his hands—the floor," said Weasel.

Georgene squirmed uncomfortably. " 'Is it smaller than a pillow?' I asked him. 'Larger than a loaf of bread?' How could he possibly tell us?"

"He tried the best he could," said Weasel.

They walked over and sat down together on the bottom step of the stairs.

"You think he'll be okay now?" asked Georgene.

She had scarcely said the words when a chill swept over the basement. Before Bernie could speak, a pale blue light appeared just over the hole in the concrete, and then the pale figure of Jonathan. He stayed for only a few seconds, but long enough for Bernie to see him smile.

"He'll be okay," he said.

ABOUT THE AUTHOR

PHYLLIS REYNOLDS NAYLOR was born in Anderson, Indiana. She spent her teenage years in Joliet, Illinois, and has also lived in Chicago and Minneapolis. She now makes her home in Bethesda, Maryland, with her husband, Rex, and their two cats, Ulysses and Marco. The Naylors have two grown sons, Jeff and Michael.

Mrs. Naylor enjoys writing many kinds of books for all ages and has more than sixty published books to her credit, including *Beetles, Lightly Toasted*; *Maudie in the Middle*; and *Night Cry*. *Bernie and the Bessledorf Ghost* is the third in the zany Bessledorf mystery series, which includes *The Mad Gasser of Bessledorf Street* and *The Bodies in the Bessledorf Hotel*.